1

Leaving Wickenburg

A fiction Novel

by

Amanda Smith

Book 1

Amanda Smith, Author
Leaving Wickenburg
Copyright © 2018 Amanda Smith

First Printing/First Edition - December 2018

ISBN: 13: 978-1-7335101-0-3

Cover Photo by William Jared Smith.
Cover Design by Amanda Smith

Self-published

Dedication

Dedicated to my Mother and my Father, who gave me the oomph to press on, and an amazing amount of unconditional love, support and encouragement.

To my Husband Jared, who never stopped (and never stops) believing in me; is my partner in every aspect of our lives, and loves me under the most trying, and best of times. You are my EVERYTHING, Professor, and I love you.

To my Twin Sister Patty and my Brother Whitney and Niece Liz - you have stood behind me, and beside me, in the good and the bad. Also, the hilarious.

To Jamie G for showing me that I can live, and ride again.

To Big Mike for more reasons than I would have room enough to write.

To Bee for motivating me, and staying on me until the final chapter was written. And then some.

To Kristie for being my cheerleader, and for the countless nights at the cabin so I could write, while you manned the Fort and the Rescue, and the Ranch.

and to Linda, for being my Soul Sister.

This book has been ten years in the making. It would still be sitting in multiple piles, on multiple shelves, were it not for each of you. Thank you.

And last but not in the slightest least, to every woman (and man) everywhere that found a new path and took it, to those who never received that chance; fly high with the Angels. And to those still looking for it, it's out there, keep looking. This book is for all of you.

Lucille was stuck in a rut; between her abusive husband, and her drinking, she had all but ceased functioning in what was left of her life, and her photography career. When her best friend Marcie of twenty years shows up at her California home, (after a particularly hard night with both of her bad habits,) Lucy has no choice but to take her up on the offer of a temporary retreat from it all. With her cat Max in tow, Lucille and Marcie load up in Marcie's old truck, and head towards a dude ranch in Arizona, for a week of relaxation and fun; both of which Lucy desperately needed.

However, unbeknownst to Marcie, Lucy had been down this road before, and the idea of encountering that part of her past again, had her heart fluttering at full speed. A photoshoot brought her to Wickenburg once before, and the job had thrown a handsome cowboy named Green right in front of her lens, and right into her heart. Although the timing was off back then, Lucy never lost the memory of Green, and how he impacted her life all those months ago. Would he still be at the ranch with those blue eyes and sexy smile? Would she be able to handle seeing him again knowing how ashamed she felt for the way her life had turned out?

Lucy wasn't sure of anything anymore, but Marcie was banking that a small dude ranch on the outskirts of a little town called Wickenburg, promised a change in the life Lucy had been leading.

Is Lucy ready to face her past, forget her present, and open herself up to a future she deserved? Only time would tell.

Lucy knew one thing for sure as she set out on the road towards a most certain "change," and that was that leaving Wickenburg this time around (at the end of what would most certainly be a long week,) wouldn't be the same as the last time she left.

If she even left at all.

Chapter 1

"Get in the damn truck, Lucille."

Those were the words Lucy heard not one minute after a flurry of gravel and wind woke her from her drunken slumber on the patio of her California home, that she loved so damn much.

"Why the hell do you have to pull into the driveway like a bat out of hell, Marcie?" Lucy mumbled to herself as her best friend came to a screeching stop in her driveway.

Lucille pressed herself up off the patio chair she was crumbled in, rubbed her eyes, and removed the wide brimmed sun hat she was wearing that shielded her still drunken eyes from the bright, and incredibly blaring San Diego morning sun.

Marcie, with perfectly curled brunette hair, hands gripping the steering wheel, just stared at Lucille out the passenger window of her truck.

"Lucille," Marcie yelled through the old truck's window. "I've been calling you all morning, you ARE going with me to Wickenburg, whether or not that asshole you call a husband, is alright with it. If you aren't packed, I'll pack for you."

After clamoring out of her truck with as much grace as a daddy long leg, Marcie waltzed past the sleepy eyed redhead, headed straight towards Lucille's old stucco home, pushed open the sliding glass door with a vengeance, and stumbled over Lucille's cat "Max."

"Crap, I'm sorry Max." Marcie mumbled as Lucille followed reluctantly behind her.
Entering into her own home, Lucille cringed at the memory of what had transpired the night before, that which had caused her to crawl her way out onto the front porch, and curl up in that ratted old patio chair as the early morning sun made its way into the sky.

"Stupid prick" Lucille said aloud.

Marcie just turned quietly towards her; arms folded against her chest and said, "Did he beat the shit out of you again, Lucille?" She asked, with no regard for tenderness. There wasn't any need for her to be tender when asking this question to Lucille, it had been asked too many times before with the same quiet response that Lucille almost always gave; a simple nod of her head.

"God, Marcie, why the hell don't I fight back? Lucille mumbled. "The cat got some mud on our carpets I cleaned yesterday, and Hank just flew off the handle again," she continued.

"There wasn't anything I could do but let him go at it, I was too tired to fight back, and he finally got bored and threw me out onto the front porch again... again." Lucille just trailed off into nothingness as Marcie grunted in disapproval, and made her way to the master bedroom.

"You never fight back, Lucille." Stated Marcie.

Lucille didn't have a response to that, because it was true. She only ever ran.

"I just love coming into this nasty-ass bedroom knowing you still sleep with that asshole." The brunette hissed as she looked around the master bedroom. "It's time for you to take control of your life, Lucille," Marcie continued through gritted teeth. "Even if it is only for five damn days," she said, as she yanked opened the closet door, and removed Lucy's suitcase from the closet's top shelf.

After tossing the suitcase onto the bed, Marcie began opening dresser drawers, pulling out various articles of clothing, socks, and under garments as Lucille leaned up against the open doorway, massaging her temples while watching her best friend pack the various items with tornado-like movements.

"Why oh WHY do I drink, Marcie? I don't know how I function properly during the day, after an entire bottle of wine."

"You don't function at all," said Marcie. "And you sure as hell drank more than a bottle of wine; I could smell you before I pulled into your drive. Now, my friend, do you want your boring-ass granny bras that hold your tits in as though you have two wildcats trying to get out of a bag on your chest? Or can I go ahead and pack these incredibly sexy, 'never worn before' bras that will make you look like the woman you seem to have forgotten that you are?"

Lucille just stared at Marcie, always mesmerized, but never surprised at her best friend of twenty year's utter brazenness.

"Well Marcie I don't really know, are the price tags still on them?" Lucille asked sarcastically. "I hate wearing scratchy bras, and that kind is always scratchy if they aren't washed first before wearing, and if the price tags are still on them then they haven't been washed, and that means they'll be scratchy, and judging by your hurricane like way

10

of packing my suitcase, I'd say we don't have enough time to wash them, soooo...better take the granny kind."

Marcie stopped for just a minute to stare back at her friend, taking note of the fresh cut on the redhead's lower lip, and the new bruise showing up just below her collar bone.

"Stupid ass always did know just where to hit her." Marcie thought to herself.

Without another word Marcie ripped off the price tags from the new and quite sexy bras and shoved them into the front zipper pocket of Lucille's suitcase. Never once taking her eyes off Lucille as she shoved them inside.

Pulling her eyes from her best friend, Marcie opened the bottom drawer to the dresser and pulled out several pair of "never before worn" panties, tore the price tags off those, and shoved them into the same compartment as the bras.

"Well Lucille, I guess you'll have to scratch, then." Marcie said matter of factly.

After throwing socks, several pairs of jeans, sweaters and a few flannel shirts into the main part of the suitcase, Marcie zipped it all up, pulled the case off the bed, looked at the now wide-eyed Lucy, and said "Ready?" and waltzed right past her, suitcase in hand.

Lucille stood there in the doorway, staring at the bed she shared with her "prick husband," shrugged her shoulders, turned towards the hallway and made her way to and out of the sliding glass front door. Max meowed behind her. Lucille turned around, bent over, picked up her over-sized Maincoon cat, and walked outside into the still entirely too bright sun.

"I'm bringing Max," she yelled as Marcie gunned the old blue and white pickup Lucille's old friend had been driving religiously for years.

"Put him in the back then, and let's go!" Marcie yelled over the rev of her engine.

After putting Max in the back seat of the old truck, Lucille climbed into the passenger side front seat and immediately propped her feet up on the dash, just like she had always done each time Marcie came to save her ass.

"Fuck it, let's go" Lucille whispered, as she looked out the passenger side window.

Both women suddenly froze as the sound of screeching tires and a second revving engine could be heard from right behind them.

"What the fuck?" Lucille yelled as Marcie tore out of the driveway.

The last thing she caught a glimpse of, as they catapulted over the curb, was the jutted jaw and angry face of her "prick husband" as he slammed the work-truck that she bought him, right into the back of Marcie's pick up. Broken glass shattered from the taillights as Marcie shoved that old truck into second and spun off down the normally quiet neighborhood street.

Lucille watched in horror as her brunette headed friend rolled her window down and waved her middle finger in the air, yelling "You son of a bitch, you have five days to get gone you mother fucker, do you hear me!!" Marcie screamed the latter so loudly, Lucille was certain it would wake up the entire neighborhood.

It was not a question, and Hank looked like the asshole that he was as he clamored out of his truck, picked up the rake he beat Lucille with the night before, and threw it at the back of Marcie's truck.

"Why in the HELL is he HOME?" Lucille seethed to her friend. "DAMMIT, NOW WHAT?" She cried as she buried her arms in the crook of her elbows, knees bent and feet still on the dash.

Lucille's head began to pound as the memory of the night before came crashing back to the forefront of her swimming mind, and before she could stop it from happening, her brain kicked into overdrive, and she began mentally re-living the night before, while Marcie angrily lit a cigarette, took a good long drag, and rumbled on down the road; heading her truck, herself, and her broken best friend, in the direction of the Arizona border.

"LUCILLE!" Hank yelled from the side door of the house that led into her home office. She had spent the day editing rodeo photos from the three rodeos she had photographed earlier in the week, had cleaned the carpets with the shampooer earlier in the morning, and was now taking a quick break to pull weeds in her flower bed. Pulling weeds always set her mind at ease, and got her creativity flowing again.

Hearing her name yelled, she forced herself into an upright position from weeding. Shielding the San Diego sun with her right hand, she squinted in the direction of her husband's all too familiar voice. "God I hate that belittling, creepy, condescending voice... of my prick husband," Lucille said to no one in particular as she slowly made her way up the short walkway to the doorway that her husband was standing in.

"Why does he always have to sound so condescending?" She said to herself as she timidly, and with growing fear, approached the shadow of the grimacing and clearly angry, short, ugly, crooked toothed man that she had married just five short years ago. Married him when she thought his height, looks and smile were of the kind of man that could fit in to her heart just fine.

Boy was she wrong.

"Did you wash the carpets today, Lucille?" Hank said. "Because they sure look clean," he continued in his condescending voice as he looked up into her eyes with that "I'm about to tell you how I really feel" look, in his eyes.

"Yes, I did Hank." Lucille couldn't hide the building trepidation in her voice. "Is everything OK?" Lucille asked as the all too familiar feelings of fear and panic began to well up inside her, along with every question she had ever asked herself before, when she knew she more than likely did something wrong, again.

"No Lucille," her husband said, as a slight smile crept across his face. "Everything is not all right." Hank turned into the office that Lucille did her most creative works in, that Hank always hated, and pointed to a few cat-like paw prints on the freshly cleaned, white carpet.

"Do you call that 'All-Right,' Lucille?" Hank grabbed Lucille's shoulders and turned her towards the paw prints. "Or, did you see those paw prints earlier and just ignore them like you do everything else in this goddamned filthy fucking house?" He said quietly through gritted teeth.

Lucille stared blankly at the two tiny paw prints on the carpet, that were most assuredly from her cat, Max. He was a big old Bobcat/ Norwegian Maincoon, weighed almost 20lbs, and was the absolute light of her life, and the one thing that made her feel safe in this world.

"I'm so sorry Hank, no I didn't see those, but I'll get them cleaned up right now."

"You need to get rid of that damned cat, Lucille."

"No Hank, I'm not getting rid of Max, not now, not ever." Lucille said to herself. Knowing full well what would happen had she voiced her thoughts out loud.

Lucille grabbed a Clorox wipe out of the bottle off the desk that her computer sat on, and got down on her hands and knees and began to scrub at the two tiny paw prints, innocently made by the only being in her life that she could love and trust; "Max."

Lucille quickly wiped at the one single tear that had escaped from her eye.

"You think it's funny, Lucille, don't you?" Hank said as he stood over the now trembling woman. "That your cat just walked pompously across the carpet that you JUST cleaned, and got it all dirty again, huh Lucille, you think it's funny, I can see it on your face" he continued. "Well, maybe I'll get rid of that cat for you, Lucille."

"No Hank, I don't think it's funny, and please don't even think of touching Max."

Anger now taking over her fear and panic, she knew she had used the wrong voice when she stated the latter. She knew before it happened, that he was going to kick her.

And then, he kicked her. Right in her side.

"Well that's a first," thought Lucille, as she grabbed her side, wincing from the sudden onset of pain. "Quite normally he just pulls me by my hair, and drags me around the house." She said to herself.

Freezing in motion, she waited for the next blow to happen, and when it didn't, she got up to run out the door, but good ol' brave Hank tripped her on the way out. As she fell forward, her face hit the corner of the desk, and she felt her lip pop open. In just as fast a motion, she pushed herself back up and continued out the office door into the side yard and grabbed a big red plastic rake that was under a chinaberry

14

tree. Not to use it against him, she knew better than that, but so that he couldn't use it against her. Hank had come after her with that big red rake in the past, and she knew that he kept it around as a quiet little reminder of just how easy it was for him to control her.

Lucy threw the rake, intending it to be tossed far enough away from her that he couldn't get to her and it, at the same time.

Talk about a backfire, the rake hit the house instead and bounced right back at her feet; and good old love-able Hank, who was seeing red now, which meant there was nothing that was going to be able to stop him, picked up that rake and with his chin jutted out, and his yellow, crooked teeth clenched together, he whacked Lucille right across the chest. Swung back like he was holding a baseball bat about to hit a home run for the World Series and WHACK, hit her again, right smack dab on her reddening chest, just below the collarbone.

"How the HELL does he hit like that?" Lucille wondered as she stood there waiting for the next blow. Hands up over her head, not that he EVER hit her in the head, it was just reaction.

"I fall and break my lip open, but he beats me with a rake and manages to hit me each and every time in an area that unless I take my shirt off for all the world to see, no one will ever see." She screamed inside her head as she braced herself in a crouching position up against the base of the tree.

WHAM another blow, this time to her right thigh. That stung. Lucille liked to wear tight jeans because it made her feel like she was a little more "put together." But when that rake hit her thigh, she wished at that very moment that she was wearing anything but.

When he was finished pummeling her with the rake, and only after she heard him climb inside the work truck she had purchased for him so he could start his own yard care business, and only after she heard him drive far, far, away, did she even dare to get up and move through the light of the setting sun, back up onto the walkway, and through her office door into the house. All the while praying to God, once again, that not a soul witnessed what had just transpired. Walking straight to the kitchen she grabbed the extra large bottle of Merlot that Hank always brought home for her, every night after work, and popped off the cork.

Tonight she didn't even start out with a glass, she just took a good long swig right out of the bottle and let the stinging sensation of that smooth and velvety deep, purple wine, burn down her throat into her chest and into her belly.

Only then did she reach for a glass, because it never really did taste as good right out of the bottle, and after all, she did like the taste of good wine.

"Well, here's to you and me, Max." Lucille said out loud as she pointed her large "filled to the rim" glass of wine towards Max, and toasted the old cat. Max stared at Lucille with his big green eyes, meowed loudly and jumped up onto the windowsill behind her.

As she took another good, long, refreshing drink of her favorite wine, she watched in horror as the hair on Max's back stood straight up; arching his back just like the cats on the Halloween decorations, he began hissing out the window.

That's when she saw his headlights pull into the driveway.

Before she knew it, good old Hank was back in the house, pissed as hell at her for not calling to see where he had gone.

"Didn't you care that I left, Lucille?" Hank stood there in the living room in front of the now opened front door.

"No, I mean... yes, Hank, I did, I just thought that you needed some space so I..."

...and that's when he leaped across the floor towards her, took a great big handful of her red locks into his hands, kicked Max across the room, and dragged her by her hair, tossing her like a rag doll out onto the front porch (of the house she bought with her own money,) and locked the door behind her.

She waited an hour until she could no longer hear a sound inside the house, crept in through the back window of the bathroom, silently made her way into the kitchen, and grabbed the remaining bottle of wine, a blanket and her favorite floppy blue and white sunhat, and snuck back outside. She sat down on the front porch and quietly leaned up against her front door, thankful that Hank had turned the porch light off, which meant that no passerby (unless they really looked,) would see her sitting there.

And she drank.

...and then she climbed up onto the patio chair that sat on the side of the house next to the kitchen window, and she drank some more.

Hoping to block out any sense of reality, she put her hat on and pulled the wide brim down over her face so that the morning sun might not wake her, and she slept until she heard good Old Hank clamoring around outside in the driveway. She stayed intensely still until she heard him get in his truck and leave. It must have been about 5am, because that was when he always left for work.

He either saw her and chose to ignore her, or he simply didn't care to look for her. Either way, he left.

Lucille fell back to sleep outside on her chair, wondering if she should instead get off her lazy, drunk ass and go get packed for a fun filled girl trip that her best friend in the whole world, wanted her to go on.

As Lucille shook herself from the end of last night's memory, she heard her best friend respond to her earlier question of "Now What?" before the memory took over.

"What do you mean "NOW WHAT?" seethed Marcie back to her surprised friend.

Lucille barely heard Marcie's initial response to her own initial question of "NOW WHAT" because she was so mesmerized by the quick two minute, terrifying memory that seemed to take an hour to swim through her consciousness.

Lucille stared ahead through the windshield as they drove down the road towards Arizona. She'd been there before, to Wickenburg; a long time ago when life was just getting complicated. She met a man there, but she was married to Hank, and there was no way she was ever, ever going to lose the trust she worked so hard to gain in that old prick.

His name was Green. That's how she referred to him whenever she talked about Wickenburg, and she only talked about Green, and Wickenburg, to herself.

Shaking herself from her thoughts once more, Lucille heard her BFF exclaim;

"We head the fuck to Wickenburg, that's WHAT." Marcie said as she stepped on the gas, flipped on the radio to a country station, and turned it up as loud as loud could be.

Turning left onto the roadway that would take them to Interstate 5, which would then take them onto I8 East to Arizona, Lucille wished to herself that her friend wouldn't say "Fuck" quite so much. Descriptive as it was.

Chapter 2

"How's your lip?" Marcie asked over the loud radio, eyes still on the road in front of her as she side glanced for just a second to see tears quietly streaming down her best friend's face.

Marcie turned off the radio and waited for her friend to respond.

"Now come on now, baby girl," Marcie said as she reached over and jostled the mop of red hair on Lucille's head. "Let's have a look," she stated as she slowed the truck down a bit.

Lucille turned her tear-stained face to Marcie and stuck out her lower lip.

"How ugly is it?" She asked Marcie. "How ugly am I?"

"You aren't ugly at all my friend, but that lip sure leaves something to be desired. There's some Kleenex in the glove box, throw a little spit on it and get the blood off, honey." Marcie said quietly as she turned her eyes back on the road in front of her.

Hank had been beating on Lucille for as long as they were married, hell— probably even before, but Marcie knew that it was fruitless to ask. Lucille would never admit to that. Not ever. Not even to Marcie. But Marcie had finally had enough, even if her best friend hadn't. When the chance came for her to join a group of women on a dude ranch for an all girls getaway, Marcie jumped on it, and told Lucille she was bringing her along for the ride.

And that's where they were headed that fine October day. To a dude ranch in the middle of Arizona, on the outskirts of a little town called Wickenburg, where it was told that lives that were shattered, apparently without knowing, could begin anew.

Marcie was on a mission, a mission to find out if even the shattered life of a beaten down, "used to be" acclaimed photographer of the west, could be put back together because of a little town called Wickenburg.

"I'm sorry about your tail-light, Marcie." Lucille said quietly as she turned to look at Marcie.

Marcie just shrugged her shoulders, and mumbled something about a war wound; and then she lit another cigarette.

Her best friend with a mane of chocolate swirls and highlights, always seemed to love Lucille, even at her worst. Lucille felt that this was probably very much her worst, because aside from the throbbing headache from too much wine, and the pain in her lip, chest and thigh, she could also feel a sort of slipping away kind of feeling in her soul.

That feeling was the same kind of feeling she felt seven years ago when she was moving a couple of cattle down a steep slope just outside of San Diego, in the Mountainous areas of the Cleveland National Forest.

And off into memory-land, Lucille went again …

She had only known Hank a few months, but they were already living together in her two-bedroom apartment on the outskirts of San Diego, the most vacationed city in America.

She could recall this same lost feeling she was experiencing now, in this truck headed for the ever famous, Grand Canyon state, as she recalled moving a pair of long horns down over some rocks, when a rattle snake came out from underneath a boulder and bit the horse she was riding on the back leg. Up and over that horse went, and up and over and off the horse, Lucille went. Landing on the rocks below she looked up just in time to see that big old beautiful red roan land right on top of her.

While her heart sank, and she wondered if she would live, she passed out at the precise moment that she felt the bottom part of her right leg, break right in half.

She healed over time; three and a half months worth of time. And she recalled, (as she and her best friend headed down the Interstate,) how those months really should have hoisted a few more red flags regarding Hank, than were already waving in front of her face at the time.

Back then Hank used to play games with her head, but they were both drinkers, and Lucille just assumed it was a way for Hank to play hard to get. She soon realized that the more she played into Hank's game of hide and seek (she would never hear from him when he went to work, and never quite knew when he'd be home from work) the more he seemed to come around, and the more time they spent together.

She was smitten. He was a rodeo cowboy who not only rode the circuit, but he also had a full time job, the same job for the last 17 years, and that was a pretty rare find these days. A real rodeo

20

cowboy. She wasn't about to let that one get away. Even if there were 52 red flags from the get go.

To make a long story short, crutches, broken leg and all, Lucille still had to go to work, and get her own self up and down the flight of 13 stairs that took her to her two bedroom, second floor apartment. She was fine with that, and she was fine with work, hell she'd worked three jobs (and put her own self through college) most of her life, nothing much phased her.

What she wasn't fine with was being expected to still have dinner cooked and ready for Hank, no matter what time he walked through the door.

Any amount of time that her leg was down, it would start throbbing so badly that her head would start to swim. When she cooked Hank's supper, she had to do so while hoisting her casted leg up on the counter-tops as she moved herself around her small, quaint apartment sized kitchen.

The same went for his breakfast. How the hell she ever decided THAT was O.K., was beyond her. She often wondered why he didn't once in awhile make her breakfast in the mornings, while her leg was shattered in three places. After all, they both worked. He always seemed to get particularly edgy back then, when she brought that up, so she left it alone.

Hank never really helped Lucille at all when her leg was broken, and try as she may to see if she was just being selfish or not, she decided that it didn't matter if he helped her out. He had a life, too, and who wants to be tied down caring for a rodeo photographer with a broken leg, who wouldn't be able to shoot the circuit this year.

You can't move very fast in a cast, and when you're in the arena with cowboys and bulls, you'd better be able to run.

Too bad she didn't take that into consideration the day Hank asked her to marry him.

In retrospect, as Lucille turned her face from the passenger side window to stare out the windshield instead, she decided that Hank probably had good reason to let her take care of her own broken leg all those years ago; and that the time she asked him why he didn't want to help her, which resulted in the first time he ever hit her, was probably just a bad time to ask him that particular question.

"You want something to eat, Lucille?" Marcie asked as she pulled the truck off the interstate and headed in the direction of a pair of golden arches.

"Where are we?" Lucille asked as she pulled her mind away from her current memory.

"We're still in California, dream-girl. About an hour from the state line of Arizona. What have you been thinking about so quiet over there in my passenger seat? And by the way, did you know Max snores?"

"Yes, I know he snores, it's one of the things I love about him," said Lucille as she uncurled herself from her "feet on the dash position" and peeked at her giant of a cat stretched out on the back seat. Stretching her legs and trying to work out the "been bent at the knees too long" kinks, Lucille decided that she was starving.

"Sure, I could use a greasy gut bomb, and a Coke. Did you happen to grab my wallet off the dresser while you were packing my shit?" Lucy asked.

"I sure did, Lucy, but you won't be needing it. This trip is on me."
And after about 15 seconds of silence, save for the rumble of the road beneath them, Marcie followed up with:

"Oh, and on Hank, too, thanks to the ten one hundred dollar bills I found in his underwear drawer." Marcie let a smile creep across her lips, as Lucille stared at her in disbelief.

Whhuuut?" Marcie said in her fabulous pretend "southern drawl" that she always did so well. "You didn't know about that money, Lucy? It was right there in the drawer below your sexy bras, on top of what seemed like a well-used porn- oh-graphical magazine." Marcie said with a smirk.

Switching back to her drawl she said "Who gives a shiyaat, Lucille, what's he gains do? Come chase us? He won't even know it's gaawwwn."

Marcie had a good point about that. Hank would gamble at the bars, and usually come home drunk. If ever he won anything, he always stashed it in his underwear drawer under those wretched, filthy magazines he thought she knew nothing about.

Hank never seemed to remember that he had stashed any money at all, because Lucille would, on occasion, hear him make a few calls to friends he had gambled with, asking them if they knew if he had won any money, because he didn't have any on him, and because he couldn't remember from the night's events before.

For the record, good ol' Hank never, ever, wore underwear. He hated wearing them because they would crawl up his crack and "put him in a bad mood." So, there was a pretty good chance that Marcie was right, and Lucille was too hungry to give a shit one way or the other.

IF she went back home, she was going to get a beating or two no matter what she did or didn't do. So, what did she have to lose?

Nothing. Not a damn thing.

"Let's hit the drive-thru, Marcie, I don't want to stop our forward motion."

Marcie placed an order of two double cheeseburgers, two large fries, two large cokes, and a large water for Lucille's dehydrated head, and they were back on their way towards Wickenburg.

Marcie honked the old truck's horn while passing the sign that said "WELCOME TO ARIZONA" and Lucille couldn't help but wonder if "Green" was still with the Dusty Bar Trails dude ranch.

The very ranch she'd met him on, and the exact ranch she and her best friend were headed to.

Not that she'd do a damn thing if she did bang into him, unless she was single. And she certainly wasn't single. No, she was very much married, to an asshole, and for whatever reason, her heart just would not allow her mind to convince her to pretend she was not married.

Chapter 3

They were taking the long way, according to Marcie, and as she turned the truck onto I10 East to Arizona and towards their destination, she finally asked Lucille to tell her about the night before.

"You need to talk about it, Lucille. You can't just sit there for the next hour, and continue to sulk."

"I know" said Lucille as she stared out at the long stretch of highway in front of them. Damn, Arizona sure has a beauty all its own, she thought to herself. A majestic sort of power that always pulled her in some way, away from all the bad she lived in.

Lucille slowly began telling her what happened; about the carpet, and Max's paw prints. As she told Marcie, step by step, what that asshole Hank did to her, good old Max climbed up through the center console, and onto Lucille's lap.

Scratching her old cat's ears, she continued telling Marcie just exactly what happened, ending her story just like all the other stories, how it was all her fault, and how if she'd of caught those damn paw prints before he came home, maybe hadn't gotten up from editing photos to weed for a bit, that she'd have seen those paw prints before Hank did. Marcie was quiet for a bit, chewing on the words that Lucille had just spoken.

And in the quiet of the lumber of Marcie's old Ford truck, Max began to purr, and Lucille began to smile, and then she began to laugh.

"Why are you laughing, Lucy? " Marcie said through her own stifled, oddly gleeful chuckle.

Lucille just laughed louder, and pretty soon Marcie couldn't contain herself either, and she began to laugh, and the two of them laughed for a full five minutes until Marcie, no longer able to control herself, pulled the truck over onto the dusty shoulder of the highway, and there they sat, laughing until Lucille started crying, which made Marcie laugh even harder, which made Lucille get a little pissed off, and then laugh some more, and then cry some more.

"I need to stretch my legs. Lucille said through a combination of laughter, sobbing, and anger, as she maneuvered Max onto Marcie's lap, swung the passenger side door open, and stepped out onto the gravel that covered the shoulder of the road they pulled onto.

Marcie, trying in vain to stifle her laughter, carefully placed all 20lbs of Max back onto the back seat, turned the ignition to the off position, and clamored out of the truck.

The air was so still you could have heard a pin drop, as Marcie's laughter dimmed into a light giggle that soon gave in to a calm the likes she had never felt before.

"Calm before the storm? Or storm before the calm?" She thought to herself as she began stretching out her tired back.

Lucille began picking up stones, one by one, and throwing them. First she was just sort of tossing them out into the sage brushed prairie that led up to the mountains she'd fallen in love with the first time she made this trek. But then she began to add a little oomph to her tossing, and started throwing the stones.

Marcie walked around to the front of the truck, as Lucille continued throwing the stones a little bit harder. Leaning up against the truck, she lit a cigarette while Lucille picked up an even bigger stone, and threw it even harder, then watched her kneel down on to the ground and pick up another stone, only this time it was more of a rock, and watched her thrust it with all her might, and then another, and another until her wild, red headed best friend was thrusting stones and screaming at the top of her lungs, wildly picking up more stones and rocks, and from her now sitting position, yelled and screamed even harder.

Marcie watched on, quietly dragging on her cigarette as her best friend of 20+ years (who had a head full of the most gorgeous red hair she'd ever seen, skin the color of ivory and eyes the color of emeralds;) turned into a wild, cursing, screaming, shell of the woman that she once was, and let it all out.

"I HATE YOU!" Lucille screamed as she picked up a handful of stones and dirt and gravel in each hand and flung it all out in front of her.

"I HATE YOU!" She screamed even louder. Only this time Marcie watched on in amazement while Lucille emphasized on the letter "I" and the word "YOU" with a sob in between each word so that it sounded more like a dying donkey screaming; EYYYYEEE HATE YOUUUUUUUUU!

"Damn, she sounds just like an Ass whose leg is caught in a trap," Marcie thought to herself as she took another long drag off of her cigarette. "I should video this," she whispered to herself.

"Lucille, keep screaming!" Marcie yelled. "I'm going to get all this on video so you can remember just how damn crazy that asshole you keep going back to makes you feel!" Marcie continued as she ran to the back of the truck, and began rummaging through her luggage.

As Marcie fumbled around in the truck for her high performance, but super small digital video camera, Lucille got up from her tantrum position, and with hands clenched at the sides of her body, neck stuck out like a rooster on crack, she screamed "ARE YOU CRAZY, MARCIE!"

Marcie turned the camera on and pointed it at the wild woman in front of her and yelled "NO I'm not crazy, Lucille! But you sure as hell are, and I'm finally going to get the chance to prove it!"

Marcie squealed as Lucille lunged at the camera, screaming obscenities at her best friend, as the brazen brunette ran backwards all the while filming the seemingly crazed redhead who was still screaming and waving her arms.

"DO YOU KNOW HOW DAMNED BEAUTIFUL YOU LOOK WHEN YOU ARE CRAZY, LUCILLE!?" Marcie yelled out to her best friend, while still videoing. "HAS HANK EVER SEEN YOU THIS WAY?" She continued yelling. "BECAUSE HE WOULD SHIT A BRICK IF HE EVER SAW HOW GREEN YOUR EYES GET WHEN YOU ARE COMING UNGLUED!"

"To hell with you, Marcie! AND TO HELL WITH HANK, TOO! TO HELL WITH HIM!" Lucille yelled into the video camera, "UP YOURS, HANK! Lucille screamed again only this time holding her middle finger as close to the lens of the video camera as she could get it. UP YOURS, YOU S.O.B! YOU STUPID, IGNORANT, UGLY JACKASS!! I HATE YOU!"

And then she did it again, she sounded just like a dying horse as she yelled one last time, eyes as wide as the Arizona sky.

"EYYEEEE HATE YOUUUUUUUUUUUUU!" Both middle fingers just a flyin'.

And with that last and final outburst, Marcie filmed Lucille falling to the ground in a fetal position, filmed as her broken and torn friend began whimpering, and filmed some more as Lucille pulled herself up onto her knees, dropped her face forward into her bleeding and dirt covered hands, and began to sob.

She sobbed like she had never sobbed before, and then she sobbed some more.

Marcie lit a cigarette with one hand and kept right on filming with the other.

To Marcie's surprise and delight, Lucille looked up from her hands, stared right at her best friend, and with her middle finger on both hands, flipped the best bird that Marcie had ever seen, right into the still filming camera, stood up, walked right up to Marcie, took the cigarette out of her surprised friend's mouth, and took a good long drag... and then exhaled.

"Where's the vodka?" she suddenly and very calmly said to Marcie, who was still filming.

"In my suitcase" Marcie said, stifling a giggle.

"Well go get it because I need a drink, and my throat hurts worse than my lip."

Marcie threw back her head, and let out a guffaw the size of Texas. Lucille hadn't heard Marcie let out a laugh that loud in years.

"Oh Lucy, when in thee HELL will you EVER learn?"
"Learn What?" Stuttered Lucy.

"You want a DRINK because your throat hurts?" Marcie shouted. "WRONG! You want a drink because you can't handle that you just cut loose for the first time in a long time, and you don't know what to do with your damn emotions; THAT'S why you want a drink!"

"Well up yours Miss Marcie, for being so poignant in pointing out the obvious. Now, are you going to get me that drink or what? Because don't tell me you don't want one right now, too."

"Oh I do, Lucy, I do" said Marcie as she turned on her heavily heeled black cowboy boot, headed for the back of the truck, popped down the tailgate, pulled a cooler out, and opened up the top.

"Here" she said as she tossed the bottle of ice cold Vodka, to Lucille. It had been nestled in her high tech cooler since she headed to her best friend's house this morning.

"Thank You" Lucille said as she smirked, twisted off the top, and took a good long drink.

Spitting the liquid out in a vehement manner, she looked incredulously at Marcie, who was smirking right back at her "still hung over" best friend.

"THIS IS WATER! STRAIGHT WATER, MARCIE!" bellowed Lucille.

"No shit, Sherlock, now get in the truck and drink up. You still look like hell, and we aren't showing up at one of the nicest dude ranches in Wickenburg, with you looking dehydrated from last night's date night with Merlot."

Lucille stared in utter disbelief at Marcie, though she knew her old friend was right. Taking another drink of the ice cold "Vodka gone Water" she realized silently that it tasted good, better than Vodka would have tasted at that moment, and she knew it. Climbing back into the truck, she propped her feet back up in "travel mode," and pressed the cold, wet bottle up against her forehead and lip, then down around her collarbone, and finally up under her shirt, against her right breast that was beginning to ache.

"He must have hit the side of my damn breast," Lucille said quietly to herself.

"What?" said Marcie.

"My breast, it's starting to feel sore"

Marcie twisted the key in the ignition, and started the truck, burning rubber and spraying gravel as she peeled off the shoulder and back onto the highway. She said absolutely nothing to her best friend for the next ten minutes.

"Why are you so quiet, Marcie?" asked Lucille.

Marcie just kept her eyes on the road, grabbed a cigarette out of the center console of her old truck, lit it, took a deep long drag, cracked open the drivers side window with a twist of her hand, and exhaled.

"Lucy," she said. "I love you so much. You have been my best friend for going on twenty plus years now; but I need to tell you right here, and right now, that A: you are married to an asshole who has abused you since God knows when, B: you are a drunk because of what your prick husband has turned you into, and last but not least C: you need to change, and when I say change, I mean you need to leave your husband, then you need to quit drinking, in that order, and then you need to change your life. You need to move somewhere, hell maybe even Wickenburg, but you need to move somewhere far away from that son of a bitch, and start your life over."

With that being said, Marcie took another long drag off of her cigarette, and passed it over to her best friend.

Lucille gently grasped the Marlboro Light 100 cig, and brought it up to her lips, careful to keep it to the right side, away from the part of her lip that was cut, and the bruise that was forming in the corner of her mouth. She inhaled deep from the shared cigarette, and then she inhaled again until she could feel the familiar burn and sting that she longed for when she drank.

Then she exhaled. A loud, obnoxiously exhaled breath that carried the smoke throughout the cab of the truck and out Marcie's window.

"I know, Marcie. I know" said Lucille as she moved her gaze away from the face of her best friend, and stared out the window at the passing cactus, trying to count how many arms were on each one, and multiplying them times the number of cacti she could see.

Lucille always counted when she was mentally spent. She could latch onto anything that offered an opportunity to be counted, and the arms on the cactus were a pretty good diversion for her as they sped by each grouping and she would count fast.

One cactus – three arms – four. One cactus – two arms – three. One cactus – one arm – two. And that's what she did as Marcie drove the truck towards one of the only places that she ever felt alive.

"I should tell Marcie I've been there before" Lucille thought to herself as she continued looking out the passenger side window, forehead pressed against the glass, counting and multiplying cactus and arms, cactus and arms, cactus and arms. Lucille counted them all until a calm began to take over her reeling mind.

As they passed the sign that said "US 60 Wickenburg / Prescott" she turned to her best friend and said it.

"I've been to Wickenburg before, Marcie. I went there to shoot a documentary a year ago. It's a good place, Marcie, and if only you knew how scary it feels to be going back."

Marcie's reaction caught Lucy a little off guard, as her best friend suddenly veered the truck over to the shoulder of US 60, slowed it to a stop, quietly shifted the gear into park, and turned to her friend and waited.

"Marcie, we are practically IN Wickenburg. I can tell you later, after we get settled."

Marcie just sat quietly, eyes unwavering from the redhead across from her.

"Oh crap, alright." Said Lucille. "But you can't interrupt me" she said as her best friend stared quietly on.

Lucille told her everything. Not so much in detail, but everything that she could remember.

"I was hired to create a sort of Lagniappe kind of documentary for some dude ranches in Arizona. Hank thought it was the biggest waste of time, and was completely against it. I was scheduled to be gone about three months, and I couldn't wait to get the hell away from him. I actually thought that perhaps the time away would heal our relationship. I was wrong."

"Anyway, my first stop was Wickenburg – a ranch called the Dusty Bar Trails, and I was scared shitless. My stay at that ranch was going to be about seven days. I showed up, checked in, and scouted out the area while being introduced to the Ranch owner and his wife. To make a long story short, I was a mess. Nervous as a wet hen, but I wanted to do the job right, and so I tried to put my fear behind me."

"Wait" Marcie interrupted. "What were you so scared of?"

"The Horses" Lucille admitted quietly. "I hadn't ridden since I broke my leg in half on that mountain-side in Cali, and I was terrified to get back up on one."

"But you're an expert rider, Lucille. I don't understand? Is that why you didn't breathe a word when Hank got rid of your horses? Because you didn't think you'd ever ride again?"

"I guess, Marcie. I guess maybe that was part of the reason. But I loved my horses, and so I think the other part was because I was too scared to fight with Hank about it. So I let them all go." And Lucille started to softly cry.

"Okay, honey, okay" said Marcie as she reached over and touched her best friend's shaking shoulder. "Don't worry about the horses, finish your story."

After a few moments of getting herself together, Lucille continued on.

"The first morning, I had to get up at oh dark thirty, get my gear together, and head out to the corrals where I was told my trusty steed would be waiting for me. So that's what I did; and there he was in all his glory, about 16 hands, and red as the desert clay. He had a white stripe on his face, ears that were a hair too big for my liking, and a look in his eyes that was just this side of human. A man wearing a cowboy hat and chaps, that I hadn't met yet, was saddling him up as I walked up to what would be my horse for the week. I asked him what his name was, and he turned to me, stuck out his hand, tipped his hat with his other hand and said, "Everyone calls me HW, for Head Wrangler, but you can call me Green." I couldn't help but laugh at that moment as I explained to him that I meant 'what was the horse's name,' and he just gave me a knowing look, and said, 'this horse's name is 'Lucky,' and you must be the photographer everyone keeps talking about." I shook his hand, and told him my name; but Marcie, when I shook his hand and looked up into his face, and into his eyes, I felt a spark I'd never, ever, felt before."

Marcie let out a laugh, interrupting the flow of Lucille's story, and then she squealed.

"That's why you never told me you'd been to Wickenburg! You met a MAN! A Gen-yoo-ein, Bonafide Cowboy!" and then Marcie squealed again.

Lucille, try as she may, couldn't stop the onset of butterflies she began feeling in her hands and in her stomach, and she couldn't help but let a wide smile creep across her face as she recalled the first moment she ever laid eyes on "Green."

Marcie jumped up and down in her seat and clapped her hands and yelled "Okay, okay, continue!" fanning her hands in front of her face, and letting out a whoosh of air.

Lucille tried to drop the smile off of her face as she continued, but she soon gave up as she recollected out loud, the story of the first time she ever stepped foot in Wickenburg.

"Oh Marcie, he was something else. Cocksure and handsome, wearing brown chaps, a kelly-green neckerchief, black cowboy hat with a Cooper's Hawk feather in it, and all. Would you believe I was immediately ashamed at what was happening in my loins? Shit I'm having that same feeling right now, just talking about him!"

Marcie squealed again but this time she didn't interrupt. She did, however, turn off the truck.

31

"I had to glue my eyes to "Lucky," and start counting the separations in the hairs that made up his mane. I couldn't even breathe! I have never experienced that feeling before!"

"Anyway, "Green" explained to me that the ranch owner (Ray) had informed him of my horse accident, and potential fear of riding again, and that he'd told Green to saddle up Lucky for me. Green said that he was their best horse, and that I must be a pretty special lady. He kind of joked with me a little and had the most amazing smile, even in the dimly lit light of dawn, I could see the laugh lines around the edges of his eyes. Marcie, Lucille continued, his EYES... they were so CRYSTAL CLEAR BLUE.

Green continued to tell me that he was the Head Wrangler on the ranch, and would be riding with me for the week. I remember feeling speechless; so I just nodded and continued counting and multiplying hairs on Lucky's mane. I think he knew I was nervous, but it was interesting, Marcie; I felt like HE was nervous TOO. Like we were both two nervous strangers with a current of electricity running between us that was SURREAL. It was crazy, Marcie, it was just crazy. Such a crazy feeling I felt that morning, I'll never forget it. I've never forgotten it. Anytime I think about it, it's like it was yesterday. It's the only memory, Marcie, that I have in my head that is solid. Every other memory I've ever made in my life is foggy. Not this one, though."

Marcie stayed quiet as her rambling best friend rambled on.

"Ugh, I'm so sorry," Lucille said to her best friend. "I always talk in so much damn detail. No wonder Hank gets so sick of me."

"Oh shut up, Lucy," said Marcie. "Quit trying to ruin the moment by bringing up that asshole's name. Now continue, I'm INTRIGUED!"

Taking a deep breath, Lucille smiled, and continued on;

"So, I got up on Lucky, then Green handed me my camera, and two long lenses, and my battery pack, and I put everything but my camera in the saddle bags. I slung my trusty Nikon up over my shoulder, and sat there while Green adjusted my stirrups. I told him I was happy to do that myself, and he said it wasn't allowed on the ranch. Marcie, when his hand brushed my leg, I shit you not, I had to look down to see if it was on fire. And he was looking up at me, Marcie. And I could NOT pull my eyes off of his."

"That's a helluva visual, Lucy." Marcie laughed.

"That does sound odd doesn't it? Like my eyeballs were on his? Weird... anyway..." and Lucille continued on.

"Damn craziest feeling in the world, Marcie. I finally pulled my eyes away, but not before I saw a smile creep across his face. It was just a little one, but it was more of a knowing smile, if that makes any sense? Then he moved over to the other side of Lucky, and adjusted my stirrup on that side, too."

"Did you look down at him again? Did he brush that leg, also?" Marcie whispered, wide eyed.

But Lucille just kept talking.

"Then Green mounted his horse, a chestnut colored mare with a black mane and tail, and asked me if I was ready. In my most sarcastic tone I said 'do I really have a choice?' but I felt so stupid Marcie because it really didn't come across as sarcastic, it came across as scared; which I was, and I knew Green could feel it. Then he said 'Can you turn that horse around or should I do it for you?' and before I knew it he was reaching down for Lucky's reigns and turning him around. Then out we went towards the opening of the corral. I could see mountains, and wide open pasture in the distance, and I figured that was where we were headed, so I told him I could take Lucky's reigns, and he handed them over to me."

Lucy stopped for a minute to take her breath and then continued: "So anyway, Lordy I say "anyway" a lot, I'll try to stop that. So anyway, crap, okay so off we went over the desert floor, we rode pretty quietly for about twenty minutes or so... and Marcie, I could hear his breathing you know? Like someone who is nervous? I was trying really hard to control my own breathing because I was sure I must have sounded like an asthmatic. Then he turned to me and stopped his horse, and so I stopped Lucky, and Green said that my first shoot was of a cowboy at sunrise. I remember just staring at him, and I finally said "Alright, soooo ... am I shooting you?" and I totally remember him laughing and saying "Well I sure hope not!" and I laughed and said "photographing" and he said "Yes Ma'am, that's what the boss said, anyway." So with the sun coming up on the opposite side of the mountains, I got down off of Lucky, and positioned this unknown cowboy so that he would be silhouetted against the horizon, then I decided he should be holding a saddle, so he took his off of his horse, and held it out on his hip all Cowboy-like, and I began to shoot. I don't think I took one single breath the entire time, and I don't think he did either." Lucille continued excitedly as Marcie continued to listen intently.

"When we were finished, and I knew I got the perfect shot, you know the one Marcie, my International Color Award winner of the cowboy holding the saddle on his hip and..."

"Holy SHIT Lucille, you mean LEAVING WICKENBURG!??? THAAAAT SHOT!?!?!?" Bellowed Marcie.

Lucille cleared her throat, as she came up out of her own fog and said, "Mmm hmmm, that's the one."

"Well I'll be damned, Lucy. THE GREEN KERCHIEF ON YOUR WALL ON THAT ROPE IN YOUR HOME OFFICE, IS THAT HIS?" Marcie questioned Lucille in her most shrill voice.

"What?" Lucille said in her most pretend surprised voice. "No! That isn't his scarf, its mine!" Lucille responded.

But it was his scarf, and it got Lucille through a lot of lonely and painful days over the past twelve or so months. Yes, the scarf belonged to Green, but she wasn't ready to let anyone in on that lifesaving secret, not even her best friend of 20+ years. Not yet, anyway.

"Listen honey," said Marcie. "I want to hear the rest of this story, but we need to get going."

"I don't think I could say much more right now, anyway, Marcie." Said Lucille. "I'm exhausted just from the little bit I have told you." And with that, Lucille took one last slug of the bottle of "Vodka gone Water," and lit herself, and her best friend, a cigarette.

Off the two drove, straight on into the quaint, rustic, and very art and western influenced town of Wickenburg, Arizona. One red head, and one brunette, in a beaten up old Ford pickup, heading out to find some solace at a dude ranch in the middle of October, for a "girls only" vay-cay.

Lucille never felt better. Well, at least over the past year, anyway.

Chapter 4

"Good Lord," Lucille said out loud. "I can't believe I'm back." She whispered as they pulled under and through the Dusty Bar Trails arch that soared above the driveway leading to the main ranch.

"I cannot believe you've been here before, and never told me, Lucy. I'm a bit pissed off about that, but I'll get over it." Marcie said as she flashed Lucille a big beautiful tooth-filled smile.

Lucille knew her best friend was just fine.

Marcie pulled up in front of the main ranch, and put the truck in park. Before they could get out of the vehicle, a tall cowboy came out of the building in front of them, and walked in their direction.

Lucille watched Marcie open her door, and step out of the truck, cross her legs at the ankles, and slide her hands in her back pockets as she measured up one side and down the other in a non-flirtatious way, the cowboy approaching them.

"Well you two must be Marcie and Lucille," said the Cowboy, as he got closer. "The rest of the ladies are here, and we've been waiting on you two, so grab your things and follow me." He said, then looked over in Lucille's direction, who had, in the interim, slid down in the passenger seat as much as she could, hoping that "Ray" wouldn't recognize her.

As the owner of the Dusty Bar Trails, and head honcho for all the employees, Ray took great pride in remembering each and every guest that ever stepped foot on his grounds. He was a tall cowboy, and he wore a ten gallon hat better than anyone else around. He remembered Lucille with particular fondness, like that of a father would have.

"Well howdy, Lucille" said Ray, as he poked his head in through the driver's side window, tipped his hat and winked.

"Are you gettin' out, or did you just come along for the ride?"

"Ohhhh, hey there, Ray" Lucille said in an unconvincing voice, as she unwrapped herself from the seat, opened the door and stepped down out of the truck.

Ray backed away from the pickup and looked up over at Lucille as she came around the backside.

"Been a little while, eh?" Ray said as he crooked his head to one side, and looked right into Lucille's eyes. "Good to see you again, young lady, yep, real good to see you again, old friend." He said.

Lucille couldn't help but feel instantly better about happening on to the grounds of this ranch again. This ranch that could have easily changed her life the last time she set foot on it, had she allowed it.

She walked right up to Ray, and straight into a pair of open arms that were ready for a greeting.

"Oh we've missed you, Lucy." He said. "You sure left a mark on this old place." With a quick squeeze, he released Lucille, and turned to Marcie.

"So this is your best friend you've been telling me about in all your emails, eh Miss Marcie?" Ray inquired towards the brunette. Lucy's jaw dropped, as her best friend just stared at the ground.

"Well, I can tell you this" Ray said, as he gave a quick look back to Lucy. "I'd of never known in a hundred years, that the broken friend you told me about, was the wild, red headed photographer that stands here now...that I met last year."

With that, Ray trekked off into the direction of the bunkhouses to unlock the doors for them. Marcie looked over at Lucille, smiled and shrugged her shoulders, and motioned for the shocked red head to follow.

"What did you tell them in your "E-mails," Marcie" Lucille said, (making quotation marks in the air with her fingers when she enunciated on the word "E-mails.") I'm assuming that you at least didn't mention my name, since "Ray" (again with the air quotes) had no idea that whatever you told him, was about me."

"Oh come on Lucille, damn it, for once don't question me. Just get your shit, and your cat, and let's go."

Lucille suddenly startled, remembering Max in the truck.

"Oh shit! Max!"

Opening the side door of the pickup, Max jumped up into her arms, causing Lucy to almost lose her footing.

"Oh Max, it's only been a few minutes for God's sake. Calm down papa" she said as she propped him up on her right hip.

She always used the word papa in an endearing way when she spoke to her animals, or any animal that she felt a connection to, for that matter. And that was pretty much every animal.

Max could carry like that for days on Lucy's hip. He never seemed to mind traveling with her, via vehicle or via Lucille's waistline. Lucille loved it because even though she never had children of her own, carrying Max like this made her kind of feel like a mama once in awhile.

Grabbing her suitcase, and shifting Max to her left hip, she followed after Marcie, who had already caught up to, and was fully engaged in, a conversation with Ray.

Walking and dragging her suitcase over the rocky dirt parking area, Lucy wondered what the hell that friend of hers was saying to Ray. She knew Marcie well enough to know that she was talking about her.

Lucille hoped, as she continued walking, that her best friend had at least remembered to tell him in her "E-Mails" that she always brought Max with her everywhere she went. Then Lucy remembered that Ray already knew this, and he already had been well acquainted with the oversized, domesticated cat currently perched on her hip.

"Hey Lucy!" she heard, as the sound of a man's voice rang in her ears. "Lucy, hold up" but Lucy just kept walking and tripping along the dirt lot, pretending not to hear him. A pit was forming in her stomach. "Shit, shit, shit, shit," she said under her breath as she continued towards the bunkhouse.

"This isn't happening, this isn't happening." She continued whispering. And just as she was remembering the sound of Green's voice, she suddenly realized it wasn't Green at all.

"Lucy, it's me! Terry!" She heard, suddenly remembering the middle aged, good looking and incredibly tall cowboy she rode with on her last day of her shoot here, last year.

"Hey Terry!" Lucy yelled, smiling over her shoulder, relief washing over her as Terry ran up, and grabbed her suitcase.

"That's not Green," she thought to herself. "I should have known it wasn't him the moment I heard my name."

"What in tarnation are you doing here, young lady? Come back for another round? Missed us too much? I didn't know you were coming! You should have told us you were going to be part of this 'gal group!"

Lucy stopped her momentum, shifted Max, and laughed. Terry wasn't a really big talker, so this onslaught of questions came as a true surprise to her.

"To be honest, Terry, I wasn't sure if I was coming or not, but, here I am" she said, summoning up a smile and some excitement in her voice.

Terry smiled and placed one very large hand on her shoulder, and led her in quiet over to the bunkhouse where Ray and Marcie were still standing, and still talking.

"I see you found Lucy, Terry" Ray said, as he smiled knowingly in her direction. "She knows the ropes, old man, remember?"

"Oh I remember this young lady" Terry said with a wide smile beneath his thick brown mustache, as he let go of Lucy's shoulder. "How could I forget?" he said quietly as he winked at Ray.

"And this here is Marcie, Miss Lucy's best friend," Ray said.

"Nice to acquaint you, Miss Marcie," Terry directed with a tip of his hat, towards the stunning brunette standing before him.

With another tip of his hat towards Lucy, and a nod towards her wide eyed friend, he placed Lucy's suitcase in the first room on the end of the bunkhouse, tipped his hat again, winked at Marcie, and walked off.

"I'll see you two gals at supper tonight." Terry said over his shoulder.

Lucille could all but feel the ooze of wanton desire coming off of her best friend as she watched her watch Terry walk away.

"Marcie," Ray interrupted, "this room next to Lucy's is yours" he said. "Unless of course you two want to bunk together?

"Oh we'll bunk together, Ray!" Lucille said just a little too boldly.

Marcie, picking up on Lucy's panic, chimed in.

"Oh sure!" Marcie stated with enthusiasm. "We planned on bunking together, if that's alright with you, Ray?"

"Well of course it is!" He said with a wide smile. And with that, Ray picked up Marcie's suitcase, and placed it in the doorway next to Lucy's.

"Marcie, it's nice to finally put a face to all those emails; and Lucy, it sure is nice to see you again, sweet lady." Said the stoutly cowboy and owner of the Dusty Bar Trails Ranch. "Viddles in an hour ladies, don't forget to wash up; we dress for supper on this ranch." Ray said with a friendly grin, and twinkle in his eyes.

Marcie and Lucy smiled as Ray tipped his hat towards the two of them, and turned to walk off, hesitating for a moment he turned back towards the women and said:

"Miss Lucy… You've got some 'splainin' to do, young lady." The older cowboy said as he walked off in the direction of the dining hall.

With both jaws dropped, neither woman was quick enough to recover with any kind of a response. They were both plenty shocked, and by the look of Ray's saunter, they knew that he knew they'd be shocked.

Lucy turned to start in on Marcie, but Marcie beat her to the punch.

"SHUSH!" whispered Marcie, as she held up her hand to Lucille's face. "Do not say another word, just zip it!" She said with a big flashy smile, albeit through gritted teeth.

Lucille reluctantly followed Marcie into the room that would be theirs for the next five days, and for the first time in a long time Lucy did just exactly what Marcie told her to do, and zipped it.

Chapter 5

An hour till supper didn't seem like much time to either woman, so Lucy put Max down on the bed she chose as hers, and Marcie began to unpack.

"You know, Lucille" Marcie started. "It's for your own good that you came here; as angry as I know you are at me right now, it's not really my fault that everyone here might know your story."

Lucille stayed quiet, and started unpacking as Marcie continued talking.

"I had no idea, I mean how could I, right? No idea at all that you had been here before, or that any of these people had any reason whatsoever to know you. I mean, God Lucy, I'm your best friend, shouldn't I know these kinds of things?" Marcie was getting a little exasperated as she hurriedly started pulling out a pair of freshly pressed jeans, and a pearl button up blouse.

"Quit saying the Lord's name in vain, Marcie, and for that matter, its time I stopped doing it, too" was all Lucille could muster up, as she continued unloading her suitcase.

"Look honey," Marcie continued. "I'll be frank, okay? I told them, and I told the gal who put this whole trip together, that you have experienced a rough time of it with your husband, and that I wanted you to come to this ranch and this "gals only vacation," so that you could find your self-worth again, and yes, maybe even the courage to leave Hank."

Marcie continued talking as she put on the pair of clean jeans, buttoned up her blouse, grabbed her brush, headed over to the mirror that hung over the one dresser that was in the room, and began to attack the knots that encapsulated her beautiful brown hair.

"I honestly didn't think it would be a big deal, Lucy" Marcie went on, wincing as she pulled out knots upon knots. "Had you TOLD me about your trip here in the first place, when was it, a year ago? I'd of never mentioned your life's history with that asshole, to anyone."

"Yes, you would have." Stated Lucille, as bluntly as she could.

Marcie turned from the mirror she was using to brush her hair in, shrugged her shoulders and in a defiant tone, said "Okay, you're right, you got me, you know me better than anyone. I would have, and I did."

"Listen, I'm not mad at you, Marcie" Lucille walked over to her sulking best friend, and placed her hand gingerly on her shoulder. "I'm not even mad that everyone here probably knows that I'm an abused woman, and a drunk."

"You're not mad?" Marcie blinked back tears from her gorgeous, big brown eyes.

"No, I'm... wait, you didn't argue the part where I said, ...and a drunk." Lucille said rather knowingly.

"I ah, you know, I really can't recall if I mentioned that. I mean, are you?" Marcie said, as she crossed her arms in front of her chest, looked right into Lucille's eyes, and then sat down on the bed.

"I don't know, Marcie." Lucille said as she sat down on her own bed opposite Marcie's, bouncing Max off the side. "Am I?"

Both women sat in silence, watching Max roam around the room checking out every smell, and every nook and cranny he might want to inspect.

"You need to get dressed, honey." Marcie said to Lucille.

Lucille got up, and grabbed a pair of jeans out of her suitcase, along with a solid red, light flannel shirt that also had pearl snap buttons, and began to dress.

"I love it when you wear red, Lucy." Marcie said, smiling at the image of her best friend dressing. "You should wear your hair down tonight."

"I can't honey" Lucy replied. "It's dirty and it's a rats nest, and I just want to go eat supper, get through all the introductions, and come back here and climb in bed."

"Okee dokee, smokey" Marcie said, as she bounced up off of her bed, and pulled her cowboy boots on. "I'm going to put on my face, little sister; come sit with me, and I'll put your eye-shadow on for you." She said as she pushed Lucy over to the mirror.

"Turn to me, little sister." Marcie said. Lucille loved it when she called her that. It always reinstated in her, just how close the friendship is that she has with her best friend.

41

As the redhead quieted down, giving in to her best friend's nurturing motives, Marcie put a set of eyes on Lucy that would stop a train.

"Don't you think that's a little much, Marcie?" Lucille said as she stared at herself in the mirror. "Not that I don't like it." She said as she batted her eyes in her reflection.

"You look perfect" Marcie said. Now put your boots back on, pull your hair out a little so you can fluff it around your face, and put these on." Marcie said as she tossed a pair of dangling diamond, turquoise, red and silver earrings to her best friend.

"I LOVE THESE! ARE YOU KIDDING ME?" Squealed Lucille. Marcie had been wearing them for as long as Lucille could remember. She always wanted her own pair but never could find them anywhere.

"Nope! Now put em on, and let's go meet the other gals, and eat some ranch chow! I am STARVING!"

Lucy agreed, and after a few pulls of her hair, she popped the earrings into the delicate holes in each of her ears, pulled on her black cowboy boots, and walked out the door arm in arm with the one and only person in the whole wide world, that she could possibly feel this comfortable with.

"Let's hit it!" Marcie said as they made their way to the dining house. Walking through the door they were greeted by an assortment of women ranging in age from mid 30's to mid 60's, all wearing the best cowgirl couture attire, that a girl could afford.

Every one of them looked incredible. Lucille and Marcie both knew that they had landed in the perfect group.

Ray walked over from the kitchen, seated the two gals in the middle of a long wooden table, and introduced them to each of the eight other women that sat on either side, and then sat down at the head of the table. Terry, dashing in freshly starched wranglers, a satiny new red neckerchief and polished boots, strolled in; and with a wink towards the head honcho, sat right across from Marcie. Ray's wife Matilda, who was dressed as handsomely as the other gals, sat to the right of Ray.

Lucy remembered the last time she ate supper at this table, Matilda telling her that she and Ray were so inseparable, that he refused to have her sit at the other end of the table like some of the other ranch wives she knew, that would sit at their respective tables, on their respective ranches. Rather, he had her seat herself right next to him at every meal. Lucille remembered Matilda's exact words "I don't like to be away from my husband that much, and I sure don't want to eat across the table from him. This way he can squeeze my knee every once in awhile."

Lucille remembered feeling deep inside her heart, that she wished that she too, could feel that way about her own husband. But she didn't. At all.

The last night at this very table over a year ago, Lucille also recalled the very strong memory of catching the staring eyes of "Green" intently watching her as Matilda talked of her own story of true love.

Lucille recalled all too willingly, the feeling in her heart she felt that night, as she stared back at Green, so many months ago.

Marcie kicked her ankle under the table, shaking her from the fog of memories that were starting to invade her mind. Lucille whispered a quick "sorry!" to her friend, and soon found herself engaging in great conversation with the many women she was surrounded by, while enjoying a fabulous supper of T-bone steak, baked beans, creamed corn, potatoes, and Iced Tea.

Although the air was light, and Lucille was quickly falling madly in love with each of the vacationing women, she couldn't help but wonder if Green was still around somewhere on this ranch. Last time she was here, he wouldn't always come for supper, likening himself to a game of pool or two in town, instead. Maybe he was playing a lonesome game of pool? Maybe he knew she was coming, (because of big mouth Marcie,) and maybe that's why he wasn't here tonight. Or, she thought to herself, amazed at her own emotions, maybe he just wasn't part of this ranch anymore and had moved on to some other place, in some other town, maybe even in some other state.

Lucille shook herself from her thoughts, and pushed Green out of her mind. She was here to find herself again. Not look for a man that would be the same man to her as he was the first time they met. Off limits. Not because he was married, because he wasn't, and never had been; but because she was married, and no matter what transpired in the shitty life she left behind for three months, a year ago, she was still married, and she was sticking to her vows; no matter what her heart told her to do.

Besides, Green wasn't even here.

As supper progressed into a dessert of the best peach cobbler she'd ever had, Lucy became more and more comfortable with everyone, and Green became a dull, (but not forgotten) ache in the most precious part of her heart. Looking around for her best friend, she caught a glimpse of her conversing with several women at the far end of the table, while occasionally making goog-ah-lee eyes at Terry, who was picking up dishes, and pouring coffee for everyone.

"Well we knew that was coming" Lucille whispered to herself as she smiled knowingly at Marcie.

Marcie always loved tall men, especially if they came complete with a pair of boots and a cowboy hat, and ESPECIALLY if they were of the Wrangling sort that worked on a ranch in a different state other than the one that Marcie lived in. Marcie wasn't the marrying kind, but she was the flirting kind; and picky as she was, it was obvious that the tall, handsome cowboy in this room might just fit her temporary needs just fine.

"He's sooooo good looking, Lucy!" Marcie whispered excitedly as she sidled up alongside her best friend and sat down beside her. Lucille was just finishing up a conversation with a few of the gals, and had just taken a slurp of the last bit of coffee in the heavy stoneware mug that she was drinking out of.

"Marcie, you slay me." Said Lucille, laughing with delight at the twinkle of a sparkle in her friend's eyes. "He is cute, and I don't see a wedding ring on his hand, either." She continued.

"He's NOT married, ANNNND he doesn't even have a GIRLFRIEND" Marcie squealed as quietly as possible, looking over her shoulder, and giving a friendly smile to Terry who couldn't seem to keep his eyes off of Marcie.

"Well good!" Lucille said. "Just promise me you won't break his heart when we leave at the end of the week, okay, Marcie?"

"Oh Lucy, give me a break, that Cowboy never has been, and never will be the settling down type, its written all over his body." Marcie gushed. "Truth be told, I think I might have found the one that breaks my heart when we leave." And with that, Marcie stood up, turned and walked over to Terry, striking up a quick conversation with him, (clearly asking a favor,) and using that charming smile of hers to coerce a positive answer. Lucille, wondering what her best friend was up to, watched as Terry nodded his head, and then tipped his hat at Marcie as she turned and walked back over to Lucille. Her charming and ever knowing smile as wide as the Arizona sky.

"He's our Wrangler tomorrow!" Marcie squealed. She always squealed when she happened upon a man that turned her head. She loved a good challenge, and Terry seemed more than up to it. Lucille was more than happy to have her best friend's new chase on her mind, instead of the occasional thought that crept in about her husband, or even more so, about Green.

"Who's up for another round of coffee, and a little story telling around a campfire?" Ray asked of the group, in his booming but gentle voice, from the center of the dining room.

Without much ado, every woman in the room stood up from their respective seats, scrambled outside, and began the short trek over to the fire pit, where a soft glow and a radiant heat was already creating the perfect ambience for a great night.

As Lucille walked towards the fire pit, she took comfort in the quiet of the night, save for the sound of the women chatting and giggling as they all made their way to stumps around the flames.

Lucille marveled, just as she did the last time she was here, that the only other sound you could hear out here, was nothing. There wasn't a well-travelled road for miles, and she loved the feeling that overcame her when she realized she couldn't and wouldn't, hear any sound of any traffic at all, for five whole days. That was a comforting thought for this rural suburban girl who boasted a country heart.

One woman, whose name was "Trish," and who Lucille had taken to during the course of the evening, walked up beside her as she was heading for her own stump to sit on by Marcie, and slipped her arm through Lucille's, steering her towards a different stump (made for two,) and struck up a conversation with her about the next day's events, and about what the horses would be like.

"You know we have to be up at the crack of dawn, right?" said Trish. "And who is Dawn anyway?" the older woman in her late 60's asked, through a chuckle. Lucille had heard that line before, and found herself laughing right along with the older and quite effervescent woman.

"Yes," Lucille said to the Trish, "I know we have to be up early and I'm looking forward to it, aren't you?" She asked.

"Well of COURSE I am!" Trish said in a rather entertaining tone. "I was just making sure YOU were." She said with a big smile through sparkling blue/green eyes.

45

"I hope I get a big horse" the older woman went on. "I love the big ones, because I'm so damn short, and it makes me feel like I'm on top of the world!" she bellowed with laughter into the night.

Lucille laughed with Trish as they both sat down on the stump together.

"Well then I hope that you've already put in a request for a big horse, Trish!" Lucille said.

"Oh I did!" said Trish.

Lucille reckoned that the boisterous but lovable woman, would more than likely get her wish.

The two of them sat in a comfortable silence, smiling as they listened to the other women trading stories of their lives, laughing and telling jokes, while Terry, who was sitting next to Marcie, softly strummed his guitar.

As the night wore on, and all the gals started to tire; Ray, Terry and Matilda stood up, graciously bid adieu to everyone, and called it a night. Lucille watched with an aching heart as the two ranch owners walked arm and arm, back to the main house.

While Terry was putting the fire out, and one by one the various women headed to their respective rooms, Marcie made her way over to the tall cowboy. Lucille had been watching the two of them converse from time to time during the night, and she felt uplifted for her friend, as she witnessed her level of comfort while Terry split his conversation up with all the women. Lucille could tell however, that he was already starting to fall for Marcie. She wasn't hard to fall for, she was a real beauty, had an incredible personality to boot, and when that woman was in her element, (and this was her element,) she shined ever more.

"What kind of horse are you hoping for, Lucille?" Trish asked, jarring Lucille from her watchful eye on Marcie. "You know you get to ride the same horse the whole five days, right?"

"I do, Trish, and I'm hoping for a horse that I can handle, and one that can handle me!" exclaimed Lucille as she silently recalled and hoped for the horse she rode last year, the one that gave her back her courage to ride, along with the gentle reassurances from Green. Yes, Lucille knew what kind of horse she was hoping for this time around, and she hoped beyond hope that she was going to get "Lucky."

With that, the two women stood up, called their goodnights out to Terry, and headed over to the bunkhouse where they made a bet between themselves, to see who would be down at the corrals first.

Lucille bent down to give her new friend a hug goodnight. Looking over the shoulder of the short, plump, but beautiful woman, she watched as Terry shook Marcie's hand goodnight, tipped his hat to her and turn towards the quarters where the wranglers lived. Marcie stood for just a second watching the tall cowboy make his way home, and then turned and headed towards Lucille and Trish.

"I just love hugs goodnight" said the older woman to Lucille, as they finished their quick embrace. "Always makes me feel like I'm hugging one of my own daughters" she said. "Well, goodnight my newfound friend, I'll race you to the corrals in the morning!"

"Goodnight, Trish!" Lucille called out to the woman as she walked over to her own room. "I'll see YOU at the corrals in the morning, when YOU show up!" Lucille said through good-natured laughter.

Lucille laughed even harder as the older woman held up her arm in the air, middle finger a flyin' and yelled, "May the best cowgirl win!" And headed to her own room in a scurrying fashion.

"What was THAT about, Lucy?" Marcie said through her own laughter.

"Oh probably the coolest older woman I've ever met" Lucille said.

"She seems like it," said Marcie. "They all seem incredible don't they?"

"God they sure do, Marcie." Lucy said as they walked arm in arm through the door to their room.

"I think this is going to be a fantastic five days, my friend." Marcie said as she climbed out of her clothes, and into her bed.

"I do believe you're right, Marcie" Lucy said as she also stripped down to nothing, and climbed in her own bed, pulling Max who was sound asleep on her pillow, down next to her side like she always did at home.

As the room grew into the kind of quiet that only two best friends could share, Lucy felt herself drifting off into a blissful sleep.

"Is he here?" Marcie quietly said from across the room, jarring Lucy from her near slumber.

"Is who here?" Lucy said, as she leaned up on one elbow and stared at her best friend.

"Mr. Green" Marcie whispered, as if saying his name out loud was sacrilegious.

"I don't think so, Marcie."

"Can you feel him?" Her best friend continued in a whisper.

"Yes, I can feel him, Marcie."
"Then he's here" her best friend said as she began to doze off to sleep.

Lucille stayed propped up on her elbow for several minutes. Quietly pondering what her best friend just whispered. A few more minutes went by before Lucille laid back down and forced herself to close her eyes. Just as she drifted off to sleep she whispered aloud but quietly, to herself; "It doesn't even matter if he is here."

"Yes it does" she heard Marcie quietly say.

"Shut up and go to sleep, Marcie"

"I can't."

"You need to"

"But I can't."

"You can tell me about Terry in the morning, now goodnight"

"Okay, thank you Lucille." Marcie whispered. "I think I really like him. Goodnight my beautiful friend."

"I can tell" Lucy said quietly. "Goodnight to you too, my incredible and wonderful best friend." Lucy could tell that her words of endearment made Marcie smile, as she snuggled in next to her fur ball of a cat, and closed her eyes.

All that could be heard as she drifted off to sleep was the soft and comforting sound of Max snoring, and the low rumble of a diesel truck in the distance. For a fleeting moment before sleep completely took her over, she remembered that the only time you'd hear a truck in the distance, was if one was pulling into the ranch.

Chapter 6

Both women woke to the sound of what Lucille knew to be the "Its time for breakfast bell," but what Marcie thought was an intrusion of would be army men pounding out a rhythm on some kind of metal device.

"That would be the signal, Marcie; that if we aren't up yet, we should be," said the sleepy redhead as she pulled herself up into a sitting position on her bed. Max rolled over on his side, opened one eye, and glared at the sleepy look on Lucille's face.

"Oh Max, go back to sleep, that bell isn't for you" she said. Max closed his eye, placed one very large paw over his whiskered face, and was soon snoring again.

"Is THAT how we are going to wake up every morning, Lucy?" the brunette said as she sat up, stretched, and swung her long legs over the side of her bed.

"Marcie it's not THAT loud." Lucy smirked.

"It's loud enough." Said Marcie as she smiled at the mop of red hair piled up high on her best friend's head.

"I don't know how you're going to get a brush through that mess this morning, Lucy." Said Marcie as she hopped up, pulled on a robe, and headed for the shower.

"Are you going to shower twice today?" Lucille said from her sitting position in the bed she found far too cozy to get up out of, just yet.

Marcie poked her head around the corner of the bathroom door and said, "I hadn't planned on it, why?"

"You might as well just do a little sponge bath, old friend." Lucy said. "You'll be plenty dusty and sweaty by the time we get back this afternoon."

"Oooh, that sounds so sexy, Lucy. I wonder if Terry will be able to tell that I haven't showered yet this morning, because I'm going to get incredibly hot and dirty today" Marcie drawled in her sweet, pretend, southern voice. Flashing a huge smile to Lucy she went back to getting ready for the day, forgoing her morning shower, as her friend suggested.

"Well Max" Lucy said to the old cat as he lay there between her feet at the bottom of the bed. "I guess I better get moving if I want to be able to get back up in the saddle."

Max just looked at the woman who had saved him from a "Cat farm" almost 16 years ago; yawned a huge tooth-filled and very tiger like yawn, stretched his paws out towards Lucy, and sat up.

It always amazed her, Lucy thought to herself, how much that cat could move her heart and her soul at the same time. Smiling to herself, she swung up out of bed, and made her way over to the dresser. Pulling the ponytail holder out of her hair proved quite the battle as she grimaced and double yanked until her red curls, splashed with hints of grey, popped out around her fair skinned head.

"Well, this is going to suck." She said as she began the task of running the brush through her hair until it fell nicely around her shoulders, making a half afro, half runway model gone crazy, circle around the back of her head.

"Shit, I really should get this professionally trimmed and styled." Lucy yelled to her friend who was just finishing up the last touches of her make-up.

"Well maybe you would, Lucy, if you weren't married to a prick who makes you feel like it just doesn't matter anymore to you if you look good or not, because HE ALWAYS makes you feel like you look like shit." Said Marcie, as she walked up behind her best friend, placed her hands on her shoulders, and turned Lucy to look in the mirror.

"Look at how beautiful you are, Lucy" she said. "Even when your hair looks like Medusa's, you are still a raving beauty with beautiful green eyes, and a raw look about you." Marcie continued talking about all the positive points about her best friend's looks as she grabbed the brush from Lucy's hands, and began smoothing out the back side of the mass of red curls bunched up entirely too closely atop her head.

"Marcie, sometimes I think I look alright, but I just can't seem to ever get past all the flaws that Hank so willingly points out to me, day after day, after day. I mean, he does have some pretty valid points." Lucy winced as Marcie began working the red mop into a thick, heavy sideways braid that soon fell across Lucy's left breast. "My nose for instance, he always makes fun of it, telling me it looks like the ski slope at Mammoth Mountain in California. I never really noticed that about my nose before he said that, Marcie," Lucy went on, "But it really is rather large and bulbous, sort of like a ski slope, actually, you know? Only every ski slope I've ever been on was beautiful."

"Honey, some people have big noses, and they are still beautiful. Now get dressed, I'm starving and I'm dying to feel movement in my pretty parts the moment I see that tall drink of water walk back into my life." Marcie said, smiling from ear to ear.

"You like him that much, after just one day, Marcie? That's unusual for you." Lucy said as she began pulling on a pair of tight blue wranglers, socks and boots.

"I do." Said Marcie. "But let's talk about that later shall we?" And with that Marcie reached into Lucy's suitcase and pulled out a handful of "scratchy bras" and said "Do you want some color under that sexy white t-shirt of yours, oh best friend o' mine? Or do you want a nude color so it looks like you're not wearing any bra at all?" said Marcie to her wide eyed best friend.

"Lucy, if I wore the one that made me look like I'm not wearing any bra at all, I'd have to tuck these babies into the saddle bags on my horse!" Lucy said and started to laugh. She walked over, studied the rainbow of colors in her best friend's hand and chose the light pink bra with the ivory straps and delicate little bow in between each cup.

"I hope these hold the girls up, today." Lucy said as she quickly put the over the shoulder boulder holder on, bent over and adjusted both breasts to be seated properly in each 32D cup.

"You'll be fabulous!" Marcie squealed with delight at the thought of her best friend taking a solid step towards her sexuality.

"Who's going to give a shit, Marcie?" Lucy laughed out loud as she pulled her white t-shirt down over her breasts.

"Oh I don't know" Marcie said nonchalantly. "There's bound to be a wrangler on this ranch that might give a shit about a pair of big breasts bouncing around beneath a white t-shirt in a pink and ivory, lacy bra."

Lucille just laughed at her best friend as her thoughts drifted away to Green. Pushing the memory of his eyes out of her mind, she applied a dab of light nude colored lip-gloss in the mirror, and turned to walk out the door.

"That's it?" Marcie said, incredulously. "You're not even going to put any make-up on?" her friend questioned.
"No, I'm going naked today, not really worried about having to look good for some unsuspecting stranger." Lucille said.

As her friend held the door open for her, and Lucille stepped out into the Arizona dusk, she wondered to herself if she had duped herself into believing that Green was nowhere to be seen, or perhaps created a case of bad luck by not applying any make-up, which almost always ensured that someone she didn't mean to see, in her unmade face, would inadvertently cross her path.

She hoped it was the latter. But the butterflies in her stomach and hands, told her otherwise.

Making their way arm in arm towards the dining house, Lucille caught a glimpse of an extra vehicle in the large dirt lot in front of the main ranch house, and stopped short, pulling Marcie to a quick stop beside her.

"SHIT." Lucy whispered.

"What?" stated Marcie as she was tugged backwards by Lucille's sudden stop.

"Shit, Shit, Shit," Lucille said as she looked in the direction of the lot, eyes steady on an old beat up red ford. The black grill guard and halogen headlights that could be seen in the hint of the rising Arizona sun, told her whose it was.

"Green" she said. Startled at the shakiness in her voice as she spoke his name.

"WHAT?" Marcie repeated. "Is that his truck?" she whispered to her friend as her eyes adjusted in the dim light, and settled on the vehicle that Lucy's eyes were glued to.

"It is." Lucille quietly said. "It's been a year, Marcie, but I'd know his truck anywhere."

"Ohhhh, shit." Was all Marcie could muster up as she pulled her friend back to reality, and guided them both towards the dining house.

"I can't go in there." Lucille stated emphatically as she stopped abruptly, just shy of the entrance to the beautifully lit dining house.

"You have to." Marcie insisted quietly.

"I don't HAVE to do anything" Lucille whispered, the sadness in her voice moving Marcie's heart the way it always moved when Lucille was emotionally affected, and Lucille being emotionally affected didn't happen very often. But when it did, it was like the air itself was affected.

"Lucille, if he's in there it will be fine. If he isn't in there, it will be fine."

"He'll think I'm stalking him."

"Are you?"

"Sort of" Lucille stated bluntly.

"Lucille, do you mean to tell me that the only reason you reluctantly got into my truck and came here, is because of a chance at seeing this man who clearly has tugged at your heart strings?" Marcie asked quietly.

"No, no, I'm married. Okay yes. Well, no. Nothing happened with Green, not much anyway. I really could care less one way or the other, I am just a little shell shocked at the moment," Lucille blurted out in a flurry of anxiety filled words.

"Then can we go please? This trip isn't just about you and whoever drove that red truck in last night."

"I thought you said this trip was ALL about me?" Lucille asked her friend.

"Just come on, Lucy. I'm starving, and I can smell the Terry from here."

"The Terry?" Lucille laughed.

"I meant the bacon, now let's go."

The two continued arm in arm in through the front doors, and were greeted joyously with loud and flavorful Good Mornings, along with one extra loud "well look what the cat dragged in" from a widely smiling, and boldly laughing older woman named Trish.

As the two women sat down at the table, they both smiled and began chatting with the other western attire dressed women that surrounded them.

"Coffee ma'am?" a soothing and mellow voice cooed over Marcie as she turned and looked into the smiling eyes of Terry.

"Well certainly, Sir" Marcie said as she held up her coffee cup, and Terry began to pour. Lucille noticed that Terry stood just close enough to press his front side into Marcie's shoulder, and Lucille also noticed the way their eyes locked for just a moment, marveling at how red Marcie's face was getting.

"Whew" Marcie whispered, kicking Lucille under the table. "Mmmm mmmm!" Lucille remarked back. "Something's hot around here." She said to no one in particular.

"BOY I'LL SAY IT IS!" said a cackling voice from the end of the table. Trish was looking at Marcie with a wide, knowing smile, while Lucille and every woman at the table started laughing the way only a group of women can laugh when a hot secret about a man, and in this case a cowboy, was about to be revealed.

And then it began.

"He's hot!" said Julie, a bright-eyed blonde from Minnesota, that was sitting next to Marcie.

"Who's hot?" Marcie exclaimed while winking at the other women.

And just like that, the personalities of each woman in the room came ringing through as the sound of stomping feet, slapping knees, and hands thumping on the table began, followed by several whoops and a whole lot of laughter.

"Sisterhood," Lucille thought to herself, as she looked at her best friend who was reveling in the limelight being cascaded upon her by the group. "Ain't nothin' quite like it." She whispered aloud, while at the same time catching a wink from her new friend Trish who was watching Lucille with quiet interest, eyes a sparklin'.

After a breakfast of scrambled eggs, bacon, sausage, gravy and biscuits was served, the table began to grow quiet, and soon only small chatter and light laughter could be heard as the women dove into the hearty, home cooked meal.

"Care for a glass of orange juice, Ma'am?"

You could have heard a pin drop as Lucy looked up into the eyes of the blonde mustached, black hat wearing cowboy, standing over her. He was holding a pitcher of orange juice in his giant, rugged hands. Hands that she had tried valiantly, for over a year, to erase from her mind.

The room felt oddly quiet as Lucille locked eyes with Green.

"Oh! Well I'd sure love some!" Trish exclaimed from the end of the table, breaking the uncomfortable silence that had enveloped the room.

Green pulled his eyes away from Lucy's, reluctantly backed away from the woman he couldn't seem to shake from his memory, and walked over to Trish.

"Orange Juice for the lady." Green said, as he poured the golden liquid into Trish's glass.

"Thank you, young man, and what would they call a handsome cowboy like you?" Trish asked the unsuspecting cowboy.

"Everyone calls him HW, for Head Wrangler" Lucille said, startling everyone including Trish, at the table.

"Not everyone" the cowboy said, as he turned and again locked his eyes on the redhead that was staring right back at him.

"Sometimes they call me Green."

The tension in the air, whether it be sexual, sensual, curious or the lot, was thick; as every woman at the table seemed to hold their breath.
"Well which is it?" Bellowed Trish, who had every intention of breaking the ice.

"Green" said the cowboy, as he continued staring into the eyes of the woman he'd let get away so many months ago.

"Well, GREEN" Trish continued. "Unlock yourself from that cowgirl and let's get a move on, Mr. Head Wrangler" emphasizing sarcastically on "Head Wrangler" with two fingers in the air making quotation marks.

Green couldn't help but laugh. Pulling his eyes away from Lucille, who was just about to pass out, he walked towards the kitchen, stopping only for a brief second to say over his shoulder "See you cowgirls down at the corrals in 15 minutes."

"I've already been down there!" Trish yelled after the cowboy. "I was waitin' on a young red headed filly that never showed up."

Lucille looked over at Trish, wide eyed. "You dirty rat, you cheated!" Lucille started to say, taking the bait that Trish offered to squash the tension that was thicker than a slab of sharp cheddar cheese.

Green turned around, looked right at Trish, and said through a quirky, cocky smile "I was waitin' too, Ma'am, 'cept a whole lot longer than five minutes after sunrise." The cowboy said as he turned and disappeared through the door to the kitchen.

"Alright, alright," Julie, the blonde sitting at the table next to Marcie said. "Do we call him HW, Head Wrangler or Green?" she questioned out loud to the other ladies. "And what is so special about a red filly that you and he have been waiting on, anyway?" You aren't expecting to ride a filly on this vacation are you?" She said to Trish.

"No" Trish laughed. "But Green sure is." And with that she let out a laugh so loud, the whole group couldn't help but join in.

Lucille was completely blown away at Trish's audacity. Or was she really just blown away at the old woman's intuition? Lucille just shook her head, decided to join in on the laughter, stood up with the rest of the ladies, and made her way out of the dining hall, arm in arm with Julie, Marcie and Trish.

"I don't know why anyone would want to ride a filly, ESPECIALLY on a dude ranch. I mean, fillies aren't really trained to ride yet are they?" Julie inquired. "I certainly wouldn't want to chance it, I mean, who wants to risk getting bucked off, or worse yet? Hurt?" she continued on with her innocent chatter.

"Well you're certainly living up to the color of your head" Marcie laughed, tugging the bewildered blonde away from Trish and Lucille, steering her in the direction of the corral that held a group of saddled up horses that looked eager to get on the move.

"Come on Julie, you can ride along with me today, and I'll explain to you, allllll about The Birds and the Bees."

"WHAT DO BIRDS AND BEES HAVE TO DO WITH ANYTHING OUT HERE?" Julie exclaimed.

"Oh boy have I got some work to do on this one." Marcie laughed to herself as the two made their way into the corrals.

Trish and Lucille were also entering the corrals, deep in conversation, and Marcie knew that she didn't need to inquire as to what the two were talking about. She knew her best friend would tell her later. Marcie decided that she would make sure that Trish and Lucille rode together, while she and her newfound friend Julie, rode with the rest of the group.

56

"And with Terry" Marcie smiled to herself. "I sure hope he really is going to be our Wrangler today.

And just as the thought of that tall, handsome cowboy entered her mind, Marcie saw him leaning up against the door that led into the tack room of the barn.

"Mornin' Miss Marcie" Terry drawled, tipping his hat and winking. "Miss Julie" he said as he tipped his hat in the direction of the 30 something blonde.

"I think he likes you" Julie whispered excitedly to Marcie.

"Well I'll be" Marcie stopped and smiled at the young woman. "Maybe you aren't so blonde after all!" she laughed.

Julie slung her arm through Marcie's, and exclaimed to the radiant brunette: "No, I'm not, but it sure is fun playing the part!" The two laughed together as they walked up to the white erase board hanging on the side of the barn that indicated which of the vacationing gals would ride what horse.

"Looks like Trish is getting Lucky." Marcie said with a frown.

"With who?" the blonde said, innocently batting her eyelashes.

"No need to worry about that board, ladies" A voice behind them boomed. Turning around they watched Green as he made his way over to them, a handful of cinches slung over his shoulder. "I'll be announcing who gets to ride who." He said as he walked up to the barn, turned around and called out to all the ladies to gather round.

"I'd like to ride Terry!" Marcie yelled, raising her hand in the air like a classroom schoolgirl.

Laughter erupted around the corrals as the ladies all gathered round Marcie, each one of them knowing instantly that they already loved this brazen, mid 40's beauty.

Chapter 7

Lucille began to make her way over to the group standing in front of Green, and consciously made sure her head was lifted high as the ever bold Trish steered her to the front of the group. Smiling up at Lucy, Trish said, "There, that's better isn't it? A front row seat!" giving Lucy an over exaggerated wink.

"How in the world does this woman have that much intuition about a woman and a man she has never even met?" Lucille thought to herself as she locked eyes with the one man who once, after a hair too much Hefeweizen beer, offered to change her life forever.

"Alright ladies, I'm going to start calling out who is riding who, so listen up."

After all the ladies giggled at once, the stout looking cowboy continued with a shake of his head, looking down at a piece of paper he was holding in his hands, as he leaned up against the side of the barn.

"Marcie, you'll be riding "Diamond Ring" for the week."

"I specifically asked for Terry, Mr. HW" Marcie stated ever so innocently, twirling her dark hair around one finger, and crossing her ankles as she stood staring at Terry, who had been watching her intently from the other side of the corrals.

The Head Wrangler continued on, ignoring Marcie with a shake of his head, the slightest smile moving across his lips.

"Trish, you'll be riding 'Big Grant' for the week." The head wrangler said.

Before he could move on to the next gal, Trish yelled out loudly "the board says I was supposed to get Lucky!" and the whole group busted out in laughter.

"I've changed my mind about who is getting Lucky this time around, Miss Trish" Green said without looking up from his paper.

Wild laughter and whoops erupted across the corrals as all the women jabbed and joked with each other about the new saying "Who was riding Who" for the week.

Green finished up his directions as each woman made her way to their respective horse. Only Lucille was left standing in front of the now serious blue-eyed cowboy looking intently at the woman in front of him.

"Hello Lucy" Green said. Not moving from his position of leaning up against the barn, his stare burning a hole in the air that was between them.

Lucille, giving in to the need to breathe, took a sharp intake of breath and as solidly as she could, said "Hello Green, it's good to see you." The butterflies began to take over, and she didn't think she was going to be able to continue to be strong for one more second.

"I switched things around a bit," he said, as Lucy continued to look directly into his eyes. "And you'll be getting Lucky this week." Lucy's heart began to race. The horse that she dreamed about as much as she dreamed about Green, was going to be hers again for another week. She couldn't contain the wide smile that instantly flashed across her ivory colored face.

As she turned from Green, and began to walk towards the horse that gave her back her spirit to ride, she suddenly stopped dead in her tracks as she realized that he said to her "You'll be getting Lucky this week," instead of how he laughingly called out each assignment to the other women as "you'll be riding so and so."

She could feel Green staring after her, and without looking back she continued to make her way to the handsome red gelding, patiently awaiting his rider for the week.

"Hey beautiful man." Lucy whispered as she softly approached Lucky. Lucky slowly turned his head, as if mesmerized by the sound of her voice he'd heard so long ago.

Lucy moved closer to the tall horse, and placed her hand on his wither, slowly sliding it up over his neck, across his jaw-line and down his nose.

"I can't believe I get to ride you again." Lucy whispered, as she placed her face next to his. Lucky let out a grumble and a sigh as he turned his head into her, moving her body closer to his in what felt to Lucy, like a hug a grandfather would give his daughter.

He was an older horse, 17 when she rode him last, so 18 now. He was spry and strong and spirited, just the way she liked her horses before her California wreck. She had never known a horse quite like

Lucky, though, and she certainly had never longed for one as much as she had this one.

"You changed me, Lucky." Lucille whispered, as a lump welled up in her throat. I wish you'd of changed me completely old man, but at least you got me courageous enough to ride again, and for that I am forever thankful," she said, her lips pressed up against his face as she quietly talked to him.

"You need a moment, Miss Lucille?" startled, she looked up and saw Terry, mounted on a big white gelding, staring softly down at her.

"Just a little bit, if you don't mind, Terry" she said, and before she could get the last word out, tears welled up in her eyes as she turned back from Terry. Burrowing her face into Lucky's soft withers, she heard Terry quietly turn away and call out to the other ladies who were already mounted and heading for the opening of the corral. The opening that she already knew would lead them into the wide open spaces of the outskirts of Wickenburg, Arizona; surrounded by a steady view of the most beautiful mountains she'd ever seen.

Muffling a sob that she, try as she may, couldn't hold back, Lucille realized if she let the flood gates open now, she might never get them closed again.

The big red gelding seemed to sense Lucille's anguish, and swinging his head back towards her again, she heard him sigh, followed by a low grumble. Looking up at the majestic animal she'd fallen in love with last year, she quickly decided that time was wasting, and if she didn't want to be a spectacle to the group for the next several days, that she had better mount up.

Lucille checked her stirrups by slapping them down a few times, ensuring that they were steady enough to hold her weight. Wiping her eyes in the crook of her elbow she took a deep breath, grabbed the horn of the saddle with her left hand, placed her left foot in the stirrup, jumped once and hoisted herself up onto the saddle; quickly remembering just how tall this wonderful animal was. Bringing the reigns up closer to her chest she looked up into the sky and was surprised to feel the familiar feeling wash over her, of wishing she'd had a flask filled with whiskey, for the ride.

"Wow," Lucille thought to herself as she turned the horse around, directing him towards the opening of the corrals. "I haven't thought about a drink since yesterday afternoon."

Still, the thought of a quick sip of burning whiskey seemed just a little too appetizing right now, and she considered for a moment getting down off of Lucky, and heading back to her room for a quick drink. She remembered however, that there wasn't a drink in her room. In fact, the closest thing to an accessible drink for Lucille at this moment, was in a bottle of Vodka in Marcie's truck, and damned if she didn't remember that it was full of H2O. Good old clear, cool, water.

With that thought, Lucille nudged Lucky forward with a soft squeeze of her boot heels into the side of the waiting horse, and moved him towards the corral opening that would lead her out into the openness of the beautiful Saguaro and Cholla cactus covered Sonoran Desert floor, surrounded by the Bradshaw and Vulture Mountains that had invaded her dreams for the last twelve plus months.

As she headed out of the corral, and out under the Dusty Bar Trails wood and metal archway sign, she reached up and touched the bottom as she passed through into the open desert.

"Just like Green did." Lucille whispered to Lucky. As if the horse understood, (and she was pretty sure he did,) Lucky nickered softly. She could feel the energy of his own desire for the desert, bolt up underneath her saddle.

"Ah to hell with it" Lucille said out loud. Letting out a whoop, she gave Lucky a strong squeeze, loosened the reigns and as his ears came back towards her, she gave the familiar click, click, click with her tongue that she knew the horse had been waiting for. As she readied herself for the wind, Lucky went from a short trot in to a full lope that steadied out into the smooth gallop she instantly recalled.

"That's the way to do it, Lucky!" She whispered to the eager horse.

Lucy leaned forward just a hair, arched her back, and let her arms move forward as she gave all the reign she could, to Lucky.

In a full sprint they rode across the familiar floor of the desert that smelled of dusty dirt, and dried cactus. Up over a short incline they slowed just enough to jump a small finger of the usually dry Hassayampa River. Today there was just enough water to cause a spraying splash as they landed just shy of the other side.

Lucille couldn't remember feeling quite so free, and by the feel of the power stroked animal beneath her, she thought Lucky was feeling just the same.

Off through the sandy floor they ran, blue sky above and not a care ahead. Heading straight for a grouping of Saguaro, Lucille let Lucky have his head as she leaned forward even more, parallel to the giant beneath her, knowing full well from past experience, that Lucky would zig zag right by each outstretched cactus.

Just as she saw Lucky's ears shoot straight up, the horse suddenly began to slow. As the horse snorted to a stop, Lucy knew instinctively to either move forward over the horses head in an uncontrolled motion of ass over tea kettle, or perform the emergency dismount she'd learned so many years ago at the Black River Farm and Ranch in Croswell, Michigan; a summer horse camp her parents sent her to every year when she was young. Without another thought she removed her boot from the left stirrup, swung her right leg behind her, and pushing her body forward she jumped with the motion of the stopping horse, still holding onto the reigns she hit the ground, legs scissoring to a stop while she pulled the left reign bringing Lucky in a tight circle back to her as he stopped.

"What the HELL was that about, old man?" Lucy exclaimed to the heavily breathing horse. Lucky turned his head to the right, as if spooked, and that was when she saw him in the distance.

A cowboy on a chestnut colored mare with a black mane and tail, sitting high atop the side of the foothills looming in front of her.

"Green!" she yelled in frustration, knowing full well she sounded as pissed off as she was. "You could have killed us both!"

Riding down towards them, a Cooper's hawk feather in his hat, she could see that familiar smile even from the distance that separated them.

"Now don't be so upset, Lucy" Green said as he stopped his horse just short of them, eyeing the raged redhead up and down. "You looked better than I imagined you would jumping off that old horse, and Lucky didn't look too bad either."

All Lucy could do was take in the laugh lines on the sides of his beautiful face, a face that haunted her for months. She couldn't help but study the blonde in his mustache, and the new red neckerchief he was wearing around his neck.

"Shit he's still so damn beautiful" she thought to herself, as she watched Green swing his leg over his saddle, and dismount.

Unable to pull her eyes away from the cowboy before her, she held her breath as he threw his reigns up over the neck of his horse. As he walked towards her, she began to shake inside, she began to shake everywhere, and that old familiar buzz in her lips she often felt when she was overly anticipated, made her feel as though she'd rather pass out than feel this way one second longer. She knew at that moment that her feelings for Green had never changed, she had hungered for him, dreamed about him, cried for him in her sleep… but she was still married… she was still married to a man who was keeping her from feeling anything at all; but try as she may, she could not become that kind of woman.

In a rush of panic and an overwhelming sense of needing to run, she quickly turned to mount Lucky; but before she could put her boot in the stirrup, Green was upon her.

Grabbing her arm, he gently turned her towards him, and in one fluid and painless moment he was cradling the sides of her face in his hands, and staring right into her eyes.

Lucy couldn't control her shaking anymore as she looked at this man she had loved for over a year. She grabbed his shirt as if hanging on for dear life, buried her head in his chest, and cried.

She cried until she couldn't stand anymore, and when he felt her knees buckle, they went down to the ground together. Holding her steady, and kneeling with her on the desert floor, he gently lifted her chin up. Green couldn't believe the sadness in her eyes, and he wondered to himself how much of this pain, he might have caused.

"Lucille, Lucille" he whispered softly, but Lucy just looked away.

"Look at me, baby; look in my eyes." He whispered.

When she heard this man that she couldn't shake, call her "Baby," Lucille slowly lifted her eyes to his, and saw for the first time in her life; real desire, and an emotion she wasn't quite sure of, but looked like love.

Her heart began beating so wildly that she was immediately thankful that they were kneeling in the Hassayampa sand.

Staring up into Green's eyes, she saw the care and concern she'd only wished her own husband would have shown her, and as Green pulled her in tight, his hands holding her head to his shoulder, she knew that she had never felt more safe in her entire life, than now.

She continued to cry, hanging on for dear life as she wrapped herself tight around Green's body. Several minutes ticked by slowly, and soon Lucy began to calm a little.

"Lucille?" Green whispered softly, his face buried in the tangle of red hair that haunted his dreams.

Regaining her composure slightly, she whispered quietly in response, "Yes, Green?"

"I can't feel my legs." Green whispered.

Lucille couldn't help but let out an unexpected laugh, aware now that she too, was beginning to feel the toll of her 40+-year-old body as they continued to kneel.

Pulling away just enough to look up at Green, (who was smiling the sweetest smile she had ever seen,) she could not suppress the laughter that was continuing to well up inside her.

"So how do we get out of this mess?" She said. A sparkle had begun to replace the sadness in her eyes.

"I'll count to three, and we'll both try to stand up." Green said through his soft smile.

"Alright, but I hope you can do most of the pulling, because I'm spent." Lucille said.

"Ready?" Green managed to say as he positioned himself by pulling his right knee up, and placing his foot firmly on the ground.

"Ready as I'll ever be." Lucille softly laughed, still sniffling from the cry she had earlier.

As she brought her left knee up and placed her foot firmly on the ground, opposite Green, he counted.

One

Two

Three!

And with a grunt he began to pull them both up in one fell swoop.
But before Lucille knew what was happening, Green pushed her over and backwards onto the sandy floor of the riverbed they had

previously landed in. Positioning himself over her body, his hands now on either side of her shoulders, he stared so intently into her eyes, that Lucille felt an overwhelming desire for him begin to creep across every fiber of her body.

Nothing else mattered to her, but this very moment. Nothing. Not her abusive husband, not her desire for alcohol, not Lucky, not anything. Except for the man who was positioned above her in such a way that made her burn with a passion she didn't even know she had.

Green continued his fervent stare, wondering to himself if she was finally ready to feel the desire he'd felt for her so long ago. Searching her eyes for any sign of stopping, his desire for her grew even stronger as he realized the wanton in her eyes.

Dropping to one elbow, pressing his body up against hers, he ran his finger across the lines of her ivory skinned face.

Breathless, she marveled at the softness of his touch, this man whose hands were made of leather.

Her heartbeat quickened, and she knew there was no going back as Green leaned ever closer, crushing his body against hers and moving his hand behind her head, bringing her body up and towards him, he lowered his mouth onto hers, hesitating for just a moment before he began to devour her with a kiss that set her passion on fire. Lucille kissed him back, hard; and Green began to separate her lips with his tongue, pressing inside her mouth, as though searching for the moment he had so long desired. Their mouths continued to crash together in perfect unison as their tongues danced a wild dance.

When Lucille, (whose eyes were closed during this unforeseen moment of such intense passion,) felt Green begin to pull away, she slowly opened them, staring wondrously into the eyes of the man she'd only dreamed about having such a powerful moment with. He was looking at her, intently. It was as though he was examining the most secret parts of her soul, and she knew he was seeing every part of her.

Green, remembering that Lucy was loyal to a fault, stopped himself from devouring the woman beneath him, and pulled them both up into a sitting position. Pulling Lucy quickly up onto his lap, he cradled her with a strength she'd never felt before, as his arms wrapped around her so tightly, that she felt he'd never let go. Lucille didn't want him to ever let go, not now, not ever. She didn't care if they ever left the very spot they sat on, horses lingering in the distance, seemingly unaware of the emotional interlude that had just transpired.

"You are all I think about," Green said, as he pulled away just enough to look at Lucille.

"I have never been able to relieve my mind of the very thought of you; you have haunted me every second, of every day since the minute you left this ranch, Lucy; and I don't think I can let you go a second time."

"Oh Green" she whispered softly, reaching up to touch his face, tracing her finger along his jawline. "You have never left my thoughts, and I have been so ashamed, but there has been nothing I could do to push your memory away."

"Did you try to push the memory of me away, Lucille?" Green asked as he looked at her intently, his eyes flashing dark, a deep contrast from the passion and softness she witnessed in them earlier, just before he took her breath away.

She looked down for a moment, toying with a tattered hole near the hem of her blue jeans.

Green lifted her chin once more, forcing her to look up at him, Lucille noticed that the softness had returned to his eyes. His beautiful, twinkling blue eyes, as blue as the Arizona sky. Eyes that were pleading for her to say otherwise.

"No, I didn't try to push your memory away, Green." She said in such a tone, that the sadness in her own voice took her by surprise. "In some ways your memory was the only thing that kept me going this past year."

"Let me take you away with me, Lucy." Green said, moving her hair back behind her ear, and tracing his fingertips across her chin, down her neck and across her collarbone.

"Let me make you feel safe again." He whispered so quietly that she questioned what she thought she just heard.

Green could see the doubt begin to raise in her eyes, so without another thought he quickly pulled her close to him, and moved his mouth over hers, this time his kiss was soft, gentle. Aware of the onset of emotions that were beginning to arouse within him again, he stopped; and with his lips barely touching hers, he said the words she longed to say herself.

"I love you" he whispered. "God knows I love you, Lucille. You are meant to be mine, and I intend to have you."

Lucille couldn't respond for the lump that was forming in her throat, she could only lean up against his chest as Green held her tightly. Her thoughts ran wild as they sat intertwined in each other, while a dry desert breeze began to move gently around them.

Chapter 8

The Arizona sun high in the sky, indicated it was noon, or somewhere close to that time. Trish and Marcie, who had broken away from the riding group to head in a little earlier from the morning ride, had been watching the scene below them unfold, as they sat on their horses far up the side of a deep wash, safely hidden from the couple in the distance.

"Well, shit." Marcie said, wiping the tears from her eyes with the sleeve of her shirt.

"You took the words right out of my mouth." said Trish, as she too, wiped away the tears that she could not keep from falling.

The two women continued snuffling as they regained their composure over the passionate and heartfelt moment they both had silently witnessed from afar.

"So what do we do now?" Marcie asked Trish.

"We wait until they get up and leave!" Trish exclaimed in an exaggerated whisper, winking at Marcie.

Suddenly they heard the creaking sound of brush nearby. Looking up they were both surprised to see Terry atop his horse, coming out from behind a huge two-armed Saguaro cactus.

"Terry!" Marcie whispered aloud, unable to contain the delight in her voice.

"Well hello ladies" the handsome cowboy drawled. "I see you're catching a little "afternoon delight." He said with a grin.

Marcie inhaled a sharp breath, at the precise time that Trish also inhaled a sharp breath. "Well, we were just, we just... oh damn, Terry... were you watching, too?" Marcie stuttered.

"I was, indeed, young lady." said Terry. "Are you surprised to see a love like that unfold?" He asked.

Trish, who was more than happy to stay quiet for the first time in a long time, was well aware that his words were directed at Miss Marcie.

"Why don't you two hang here for awhile, I'll go take the attention off of those two love birds down there." Trish said as she moved her horse forward and away from Marcie and Terry, and headed out over the wash towards the main ranch.

As the brunette waved goodbye to the old gal, Terry moved his horse towards Marcie, and Marcie could scarcely breathe.

"Do you always spy on your best friend?" Terry asked the blushing woman.

"Any time I can." she whispered. The two locked eyes, and for a moment both of them felt a spark light up between them. Marcie thought that she saw in his eyes, something more than the familiar desire she was used to seeing in other men's eyes.

"Marcie, would you like to get to know me better?" He said.

Marcie thought for a moment, smiled her huge smile, batted her eyelashes at the unsuspecting cowboy in front of her and said "Why Rhett, don't you mean to say that you'd like to get to know me better?" She said in her best, slow pretend southern drawl.

Terry, without taking his eyes off the raven beauty in front of him, let out a low chuckle, and stated simply "Now Scarlett, if I'd of told you I'd like to get to know you better, I'd of played out my cards now wouldn't have I?" he said as he gave the still smiling woman a wink.

"Yes, I believe you would have, Terry." She said as she turned her horse towards the main ranch.

"Did I scare you off, Miss Scarlett?" Terry said in a tone that was as sensual sounding as anything she had ever heard before, as he steadied his horse to remain still.

"No sir, Rhett." She said, continuing the name game as she moved her horse away, preparing for a canter. "I just wanted to see if you'd follow me without my asking."

Before Marcie could dig her heels in and get her horse up to speed, Terry was upon her in seconds, moving his horse up to her so quickly that Marcie couldn't help but pull up. Within seconds she regained her composure, gave her horse another quick nudge in the belly, and started off over the desert floor at a quick gallop. Terry pursued her like he was about to rope a steer, and as he came up beside her, he reached over in one smooth movement, grabbed her reigns and pulled her horse and his, up to a stop.

69

"You aren't going to get away that easy, Miss Marcie, and I sure don't like to play hard to get, though I'd play it with you."

And with that he was off horse in two seconds, pulling Marcie down off of hers until she was standing in front of him, both horses on either side steadying their heavy breathing from the quick and unexpected run.

Terry didn't have to do anything but wrap his arms around Marcie, who didn't hold back for anything as he pulled her towards him. Their mouths crashed together in a passion that was loaded full of smoke and fire, and a movement in her heart she didn't recognize. She didn't care to stop her heart from beating wildly, she felt her entire soul open up to this man as she wrapped her arms around his neck, and while the gentle warmth of the Arizona breeze surrounded them, she gave him everything she had in the return of her own fiery filled kiss.

Terry, entwining his hands in her hair, pulled her head gently back, and looked deep into her eyes.

"I'll take that as a yes." Terry whispered, as he searched her eyes for the answer he already knew.

"Oh I would definitely like to get to know you better, Terry." Marcie whispered as she locked her eyes on his.

"That's good." he said as he lowered his lips to hers once more. "That's real good." and this time his kiss was long and beautiful, and gentle.

Suddenly realizing it was almost lunch time, Marcie slowly pulled herself from Terry's embrace, and with a reluctant tone quietly said "I don't want to leave this spot, not ever, Terry; but I came here for Lucille, so we'd better get back."

The tall cowboy just looked deep into her eyes, studying the beauty of the woman before him. "You are a good friend to that red headed filly, Miss Marcie, and yes we should head back; but you are a woman that I would very much like to ride with again." He said quietly, his eyes locked intently on hers.

"Just say when, Cowboy." she whispered, as a knowing smile crept across her beautiful lips.

In response to Marcie's wit, Terry turned the smiling brunette loose with a quick kiss to the nose. Spinning her around towards her horse, he swatted her on her rear, then quickly boosted her up into her

70

stirrup, and up onto her saddle. Before she could even get her right foot in the other stirrup, he was up on his own horse, intently watching her again.

"Diamond Ring likes you, Miss Marcie." The Cowboy said, as he slowly turned his horse towards the wash that would lead them towards the main ranch.

Marcie followed and eventually brought her horse up to Terry's. She liked that he stayed slow so she could ride beside him. She always hated it when a man she was riding with would ride way up in front of her, like a show-off. It was a huge turn-off, and she usually would spin her horse around and head back to wherever it was they came from; unbeknownst to the chauvinist, who would all too often turn his horse around and see nothing but the back end of her horse in the distance, never to be heard from again.

"Is Miss Lucy still married to that Monster?" Terry asked the surprised Marcie.

Seeing the look on her face, Terry knew she wondered just how much he knew.

"Green and I go way back," he continued. "After Lucy left last year, he tried to find her, but the ranch manager refused to give him her information. After locating her photography website, he called a few friends he knew on the rodeo circuit, and got an earful about how badly her husband treated her." Terry stopped his conversation for a minute, and looked at Marcie.

"Yes, she is still married to that monster." Was all that Marcie could muster. She knew how private her best friend was, and she wasn't sure how Lucy would feel knowing that Green, and now Terry, had already known of the abuse.

"I can't condone an affair, Miss Marcie; but I can sure tell love when I see it, and that cowboy loves, without a doubt, that redheaded filly friend of yours" he said.

The two quietly continued their ride up and over the wash towards the main ranch; the afternoon sun hot on their backs.

"That was love that I saw between Green and Lucy back there, Terry. Right or wrong, it was love." Marcie said, breaking the silence as they continued out over the dusty desert floor. She could see the Dusty Bar Trails arch nearing in the distance, and although she wished it was still farther away, she couldn't help but want to get back to her friend.

"Not to mention," she said quietly to herself. "I'm so hungry I could eat a horse."

Riding on in silence, Terry noted to himself how comfortable he felt with this beauty he barely knew. Try as he may, he couldn't recall the last time he felt this at ease with a woman.

As they neared the arch and then went under it, continuing on past the row of cottonwood trees that fenced off the desert from the ranch, he knew that Marcie was right. He saw it too, the undeniable look of true love, as his memory recalled the scene earlier of his friend and the mysterious woman that had a hold of Green's heart.

Terry brought his horse up to the first tie ring on the side of the corral that the horses were stationed at every morning. Dismounting, he watched Marcie as she moved her horse next to his, and swung herself down from the chocolate colored gelding he had hand picked for her himself.

"Terry?" Marcie said as she came around to his side. Touching his arm she quietly said, "Lucy isn't a bad woman, she isn't a cheater, I don't know that she ever has done anything but throw away chances time and again, just to maintain the vows she took with Hank."

"So that's his name?" was all Terry could say as he steadied his gaze on hers. "This man that has single handedly all but destroyed that beautiful redhead you call your best friend?"

"Yes, his name is Hank." Marcie stuttered, realizing with embarrassment that she somehow felt responsible that her best friend never left her abuser.

"I, I've told her for years... you know, to leave that..." Terry reached up and brushed a tear that had escaped from Marcie's eyes.

"Shhh," he said quietly. "It wasn't your responsibility, it was and is Lucy's." He said, interrupting her quiet attempt at excuses for why her Lucy was still hanging on to such a man. "We all fell in love with her last year, Marcie, and we all want her to be happy."

Marcie felt she understood what Terry was saying. Smiling up at him she said, "Do you think they will still let us eat some lunch?" she said, laughing as her eyes lit up at the thought of a good meal.

"We are at the tail end of lunch, he said, but I think they'll let us eat, so long as they've saved us some." He laughed.

Chapter 9

As Terry and Marcie walked together into the dining hall, Trish was the first one to speak up. "Well get on over here and start on some of this grub, you two!" she laughed as she pulled out a chair on either side of her.

The two took their seats while the gals at the table started passing them plates of various home cooked lunch items, from grilled hamburgers to all the fixings.

"Where's that crazy friend o' mine?" Marcie said to Julie, who was passing her a plate of buns.

"She went to grab her camera, said she'd be right back." Julie said with a wink. Green was of course, nowhere to be seen.

"Ahh of course," Marcie drawled. "The ol' go get the camera trick." And everyone at the table laughed.

"Where were you two?" Debbie, a grey haired but younger looking woman asked Marcie and Terry.

"Gone with the Wind." Terry said as Marcie choked on the tea she had just taken a giant gulp of.

"Rhett and Scarlett!" Cackled Trish as the other woman looked around at each other smiling.

"Everyone knows." Marcie thought to herself, as Terry attempted to kick her under the table.

"That's my ankle you're kicking there, Cowboy" Julie, who was seated next to Marcie, said as Terry blushed, repositioned himself and gave Marcie a good kick on her ankle.

"Excellent, you got the right ankle this time!" Marcie laughed.

Marcie and Terry devoured their hamburgers, fries, and potato salad just as Green walked in to start clearing the table.

"Well hey there partner." Terry drawled. "Is Red far behind?" He continued.

Green looked Terry straight in the eye as a smile crept across his lips that were buried beneath his blonde mustache. "She'll be here in a minute, old man."

"Good, that's real good" Terry said as he grabbed his plate and Marcie's, stood up and began to help clear the table. Marcie quickly sprang up, grabbed the remaining dishes from the table, and followed Terry back into the kitchen.

"Ah thank you, mi lady" Terry tipped his hat, and winked at Marcie as she placed the dishes in the steel sink.

"My pleasure, Cowboy" Marcie said as she quickly stood on her tip toes and gave Terry a quick peck on the cheek.

"I'm heading to my bunkhouse for a spell, Terry, I am hoping to catch Lucy when and IF she comes in to rest before the afternoon ride."
"I think that's a grand idea, Miss Marcie" Terry said as he swooped Marcie into his arms, and gave her a long and deep kiss.

"Now git gone" he said as he slapped her on the rear end, and sent her in the direction of the doors that would lead her outside to her bunkhouse.

"All right ladies now giddy up and git gone" Green said to the remaining women in the dining room. "We'll be mounting for the afternoon ride in two hours, so go do whatever it is that women do, and I'll see you at the corrals at 3pm." He said, as he sauntered through the swinging doors that led into the kitchen.

Lucille made her entrance just as the ladies were exiting the dining house. She felt herself blush as she realized she was too late for lunch. "Hey Miss Elusive" Trish said as she beamed up into Lucille's eyes. "Hey Miss Trish" Lucille responded in a tender tone. "Bet you're sorry you missed lunch, my friend" the older woman said as she slung her arm through Lucille's and they began to walk. "I'm starving" said the red head.

"And I'm intuitive!" Trish said through laughter as she stopped and reached into her pocket of her light denim jacket, pulled out a hamburger wrapped in a napkin, and handed it to Lucy.

"Never say I've never done anything for you, little lady, and never let your mind wander so much that you forget to eat" Trish said to the unsuspecting redhead.

74

"Now do as your Mother says, and go eat that burger, quit thinking about drinking, and go on and get ready for the afternoon ride" And with that, Trish patted the wide eyed and blushing woman right on the ass and said "race ya!" and took off at a waddle towards the bunkhouses, cackling all the way.

Lucille stood in complete and quiet disbelief as she watched the all too knowing woman move off into the distance. "Stop thinking about drinking? But...how does she know?"

Several seconds ticked by before Lucille remembered the hamburger she was still holding in her hand. She savored every bite as she slowly made her way back to her own bunk house, still mesmerized by the words Trish had so nonchalantly spoken.

It was true, Lucille thought to herself. She had been thinking about finding a way to grab a quick drink. Any time she felt any kind of emotion (good or bad,) she felt the need to squash it; and a good stiff drink always did the trick, followed by several more quick drinks.

Drinking, to Lucille, was like Lays Potato Chips to the average Joe. When she started, she could never have just one. Ever.

After her interlude with Green, out on the morning ride, Lucille was so overcome with emotions that she asked Green to let her ride back to the corrals by herself. Green understood her need for space after such a powerful moment, and loped his horse on up ahead of her, knowing that lunch would be on the table by now, so that she could come in on her own.

When Lucille could no longer see Green in the distance, she squeezed Lucky into a walk, and slowly made her way back through the water carved twists and turns of the Hassayampa floor. It was as if Lucky understood her need for time at that moment, and rather than throwing his head and making a beeline back to the corrals, it seemed as though he purposefully maintained the pace of a snail, while the woman he entrusted atop him, felt tears start streaming down her face.

She wasn't sure if she was quietly weeping because of the array of emotions she was feeling, or because she had crossed the line and broken the vows she so desperately tried to keep.

She felt herself marvel at the sudden onslaught of guilt rising up inside her chest. It was a very real feeling, one she felt often whenever she had made yet another decision to leave Hank. That very feeling welling up inside her now, was the same heavy, heart wrenching feeling she experienced every time she started to pack her bags. What the hell was it about Hank, that made him so damn hard to leave? She wondered to herself as Lucky continued on towards the corrals. Lucille wracked her brain for one reason, just one tiny little reason for staying with a man that caused her so much confusion, pain, and sadness. And just like always, she began recalling the good times they had in the beginning of their relationship, the love she really did truly feel for him back then, the way he seemed to connect with her, as though they were both in sync.

She recalled his funny sense of humor, his ability to connect with almost anyone, no matter what class they came from. He was the first to shake a hand after a bar fight, always coming out the good guy, and the first to put reason into things that had no reason. She used to think that his waters ran deep, that he was an old soul, and she was the one woman that could make his life complete.

Those were the things that she recalled that would stop her from leaving, each time things got out of hand. Those were the memories she hung onto when she decided to cancel that time she had filed for divorce, and those were the thoughts that made her believe that she couldn't live without him. That she would never be able to be good enough for any other man, especially if she couldn't ever be good enough for this one. The one thing she buried back in her mind, the one that she had conveniently convinced herself wasn't a red flag, was that he had already been married three times before her. And still, she felt she could be the one for him.

She was not.
Never had been. Never would be.
And still she tried.

She tried valiantly over the years to get back to those moments when their relationship was new, but no matter how hard she tried, Hank just got more and more overwhelming, more and more passively controlling, and more and more abusive. She always blamed it on herself. She always felt that if she could somehow change, get back to whatever it was he used to love about her, find that one moment before everything started to fall apart, that perhaps things would get better again. She knew she was no peach herself, but she also knew that she, at the very least, didn't deserve the abuse.

Nothing ever got better, though, and because nothing ever got better, she clung to her memories; so much so, that they quickly and unknowingly, became her identity. But this time her memories had a bit of a tinge to them. This time, as she neared closer to the corrals, she finally allowed the "other factor" into the equation of all those good times. A factor that she had deliberately chosen to ignore all these years. The factor that out of all the memories she had, of any of the good times with Hank, every single one of them almost always included alcohol. And a whole lot of it.

Ray was at the corrals when Lucille rode in, motioning for her to bring Lucky to him. "Go ahead and dismount, Miss Lucy, I'll take Lucky from here. The afternoon ride is in two hours, young lady, and the rest of the girls are just finishing up lunch, so you've got some time if you want go grab a burger." he said as he took the reins from Lucille.

Lucille dismounted, gave Lucky a quick kiss and a pat on his withers, and began walking towards her bunkhouse to wash up before making a quick run to the dining house. Thankful that Ray seemed to be in his own world, rather than strike up any conversation, she took the time to reflect a little more on her thoughts, and the odd sense of weightlessness that she was experiencing, (vs the guilty feelings she had been riddled with earlier,) as she made her way to the bunkhouse to wash up, before heading over to the dining hall.

After Lucille finished her burger that Trish had so generously saved for her, she put her reflections of the happenings on this morning's ride behind her, and made her way back to the bunkhouse, hoping that Marcie would be there. She had so much to tell her best friend, the only person in her life who could possibly help her feel less guilty about her newfound feeling of weightlessness.

Chapter 10

Opening the bunkhouse door, Lucille walked into her room greeted by Marcie who had been waiting "impatiently" on her bed, for this very moment.

"Spill it, sister" Marcie said to Lucille, as the redhead made her way to her own bed, sat down with her legs dangling off the side, took a deep breath and told her every single thing about her morning with Green; that her best friend (unbeknownst to Lucille,) already knew.

Marcie never said a word as she listened to her Lucy go over every detail of what happened on the desert floor this morning, nodding her head at all the right moments, and squealing in delight as Lucille told her about the emotional and sensual feelings she felt with Green.

After Lucille was done talking, she leaned back on her bed, patting the lilac colored chenille bedspread to call Max up to her, scratching him behind the ears for awhile as he laid down on top of her.

Lucille continued

"And then I waltzed into the dining hall as everyone was leaving, and Trish gave me a burger and you know what? Don't guess, I'll tell you," Lucille rambled on about how Trish told her to "quit thinking about drinking."

"She really is quite intuitive, you know" Marcie said. "I mean, it's like she's related to you somehow, or maybe you two were special souls to each other in another time"

"I know" Lucille said as she stared up at the ceiling and smiled. "I think I could learn a thing or two from her about myself."

"Because your best friend telling you the same things isn't good enough?" Marcie said as she leaned up on one elbow and looked at her friend.

"Oh no, no, Marcie" Lucille said as she turned her head to look at her. "It's not like that at all, honey. It's just weird that she seems to know all the same things you do about me."

"Well I've never even met her before this week" Marcie said in a quiet defending tone.

"I know, I know" Lucille said in a comforting tone to Marcie. "Who knows? Maybe we were created from the same cloth?"

"Well if you were, then they broke that mold when you two were born!" Marcie said with a wide smile.

Lucy laughed and said, "I really like her."

"I do, too, Lucy."

The two sat in silence for awhile, gathering their thoughts about them as the minutes ticked by.

"Welp!" Marcie said, breaking the always comfortable silence between the two. "I guess we better get ready for the afternoon ride, my beautiful friend."

"Yes indeed, we'd better!" Lucille said in response.

"Are you changing your clothes, oh best friend o' mine?" Marcie asked the smiling redhead."

"Well I don't know, Miss Marcie, are you?"

"I should." the brunette smiled coyly. "I mean, if Terry and I end up separated from the rest of the group for some reason, like maybe a typhoon comes and we all have to scatter, and then he drags me off my horse again, and it's raining like crazy and my t-shirt gets soaking wet, and ..."

"You should absolutely, positively, at the very least, change your bra" Lucille said, laughing as she pushed herself up and off of her bed, Max jumping to the side and readjusting himself on the pillow.

"And its 'Monsoon'" Lucy muttered as she made her way to the dresser mirror, applied a light neutral colored gloss, and ran a puff brush over her face to thin the shine down.

"Oh Lucy, that man does things to my insides that I never even known I could feel before!" Marcie said.

"And what about your heart, Marce? Does he move you there in ways you've never felt before?" Lucille asked while watching for her reaction through the reflection in the mirror.

"Lucy, sometimes when I look at him, my heart feels so much, that it hurts. Not in a bad way, it's just so foreign for me to FEEL in my heart — you know what I mean?"

"I do" Lucille quietly said while waiting for her friend to finish speaking, knowing it was Marcie's turn to spill her own can of beans.

"I think, no …. I don't think" Marcie began.

"Not very often" Lucille said, knowing that Marcie would take her humor as a hint to continue on.

"Ha!" Marcie laughed. "Oh to heck with it, Lucy … I am 100% madly in love with Terry. I cannot shake him, I don't even want to, if he asked me to marry him before we leave this ranch, I would absolutely say YES."

"YOU WOULD?" Lucy said a little too loudly.

"Does that sound crazy?" Marcie asked Lucy.

"Crazier than a bull's ass at fly time, Marce!" Lucy said as she laughed at the idea that her best friend might actually really be in love.

"I can't help it!" Marcie squealed. "I just can't … I mean, I cannot even bear to think about leaving this ranch without him. I want to stay here, or I want him to get in my truck and come home with me. One thing is for certain, Lucy; I am not leaving without him, and if he can't come with me, then I'm not leaving without him."

"'Can't' come with you vs 'won't' come with you, Marce?" Lucy inquired.

"He loves me too, Lucy. He told me he does. And I think, I mean, I hope… no, no its real … What I can't wrap my head around, is knowing if this is all too soon, Lucy? I mean, is it?"

"You know what I have realized in the last little while, Marcie? I've realized that 'Love' at our age… is never 'too soon'" Lucy said — smiling a soft smile to her friend as she turned from the mirror, walked across the room and seated herself next to her best friend.

"Especially when its right." Lucy continued.

"Well how on earth do you ever know if it's right, Lucy?"

"Well, we're both almost 50" Lucille said. "And Lord knows we've both had our share of bullshit in relationships. So, at this point, who cares how you know if it's right or not? Roll with it and see where the hell this crazy road takes you, my friend."

"You act like 50 is the end of the road for us." Marcie said to the still smiling redhead.

"It is if you we don't make some serious changes before we leave this ranch in two days, honey. I for one, know for sure, that if I don't find a way to leave Hank, I won't make it to 51." Lucille said as the smile slowly dropped from her face.

Marcie could tell that Lucy was about to drop down into a depressive mood, so in order to lighten the onset of sudden negativity, she stood up and exclaimed "You are sooooo damn right Lucy, lets both change our lives. Lets both take a leap of faith together, and see where our new paths lead." Inhaling a deep breath, she headed for the door, signaling with a wave of her hand for Lucy to follow, she continued with an air of positivity "Alrighty then! I need a smoke, let's go outside and take a few drags before its time to saddle up, sugar pot pie." Marcie always used terms of endearment when the atmosphere between she and Lucy needed redirecting.

"Good idea, Marce, I could sure use one."

The two went out onto the small front porch made of slabs of old grey wood and sat down on the stoop. Marcie pulled a cigarette out of the pack in her front pocket of her shirt, lit it up, took a drag and passed it over to Lucille, who in turn took a long drag, and then exhaled as she looked out over the ranch.

"I could live here, Marce" she said.

"Maybe you will." Marcie responded as she held up two fingers indicating she wanted Lucy to pass the cigarette.

Lucy passed the smoke to Marcie and said, "do you think there is anything in that house of mine that I can't live without?" Lucy quietly asked the brunette.

"Nope" Marcie responded as she took the cig from Lucy, placed it between her lips and inhaled. "Hence my not giving two shits that you wanted to bring that giant of a fur ball you call a cat, with us when we left that godforsaken place of yours."

Both girls grew quiet, and as if on cue a loud boisterous voice could be heard from the room next to theirs as a door opened, and Trish came out singing:

"Move 'em on, head 'em up
Head 'em up, move 'em on
Move 'em on, head 'em up, raaawwwhiiiiide!

Yeeeehaw ladies, let's go get this shit over with, I'm ready for cocktail hour, and the sooner we ride, the sooner we drink!" Trish exclaimed with a huge smile and twinkling eyes.

"Well, we (Trish used two fingers to point from her eyes to Marcie's eyes) shall drink, but not you" Trish said as she then pointed her two fingers towards Lucy. "You shall drink tea!"

Lucy and Marcie both laughed, stood up, linked arms with the older jovial woman, and headed off in the direction of the corrals, where the other ladies in the group were already brushing out the manes and tails of their saddled horses.

"Raring to go, you three?" Blue eyed, blonde Julie said gleefully to the trio as they approached their respective horses.

"That we are!" Lucy and Marcie both said at the same time.

"Let's do this, ladies!" Deb yelled from her horse across the corrals. "I'm raring to go, too!"

"Woot!" Lucille let out a whoop and hoisted herself up onto Lucky.

As the other ladies all mounted, and Terry and Green rode up to take the lead out of the corrals, Terry yelled "Rawhide ladies!" and off the group went; out the corrals, under the Dusty Bar Trails sign, (each one of them taking their turn at touching their fingertips to it,) then off they rode into the wide expanses of the open desert.

Green and Terry led the way through winding draws and towering Saguaro cactus, as the ladies grouped together, chatting about keeping in touch with each other after the week comes to a close, and decidedly stating that they would all trade contact information tonight during appetizers.

Both cowboys still in the lead, took the group up the side of a mountain where hundreds of cacti could be seen as far as the eye could see.

After all the ladies got their fill of taking photos of the amazing scene before them, and cussing and discussing about what tomorrow morning's breakfast ride would be like, Terry and Green took them all back down off the side of the mountain, winding down through patches of cholla cactus, at which point each gal erupted into pronouncing the cactus' name as loudly as can be, "Cholla!" Each gal said, and then broke into laughter.

None of them could understand why they all thought that was so funny to say, but it was, and that was that.

Once back on level ground, the group headed back towards the corrals, singing "Happy Trails to youuuuuuuu". The air was full of life for everyone, as each person on the ride felt an uncanny sense of positive energy flowing from one another. As they rode into the ranch, and dismounted their faithful steeds, their moods only got better.

"Ladies, we've got your horses — y'all go ahead and get cleaned up for appetizer hour, it's gonna be a good one!" Sam, (a female Wrangler who had been gone for most of the week,) gleefully said to the group, as she and Terry and Green began unsaddling each horse.

"Sam!" Lucy yelled over to the beautiful southern teenager. "You're back!" She continued with a huge smile, then walked right over to the beautiful blonde Wrangler, and gave her a big squeeze.

"Yes ma'am I am!" Sam said back. "I heard through the grapevine that you were back, too, its so very good to see you, my friend. You have been missed." Sam said in her easy drawl. "And I'll be joining y'all for happy hour, as well!"

"That'll be great, my friend, see you then!" Lucy said as she handed off her horse to Sam, gave her a quick peck on the cheek, and bounced off in the direction of her bunkhouse.

"Where you goin' so fast, Red?" Lucille heard Green say.

Lucy felt her heart flutter as she turned around to see the man she loved, watching her intently. His steel blue eyes combing over every inch of her body in such a way that she began to feel heat in places that were already a little too hot for her liking.

"Well I'm going to get cleaned up so I look fancy for you at appetizer hour, Green" Lucy said while batting her eyelashes. "You'll be there won't you?" She continued, surprised at her own brazenness.

"Wouldn't miss sharing an evening with you for the world, Red. See you there, beautiful." Green said as he winked at Lucille, and then willed his eyes away from hers so that he could finish his task at hand.

Marcie, Trish, Deb, Julie and the gang were already arm in arm heading out of the corrals as Lucille rushed up to them, entwining her own arm through Trish's, who, without even looking, stuck out her elbow as if knowing the exact moment that Lucille would hook up.

Skipping and laughing like school girls, the group began to separate as they neared their respective rooms, and one by one each lady said they'd see each other for hors d' oeuvres within the hour, after getting cleaned up.

"Don't forget we dress for supper, ladies!" The group heard Ray, (who was walking across the grounds carrying a tray of ribs,) yell as he went in through the back door of the kitchen.

"Yes sir!" Each lady yelled as they all made their way into their rooms, and shut their doors.

"Woooo-ooooo-ooooot!" Lucy said as she dropped down onto her bed and began pulling off her boots.

"Woooooot!" is right, my beautiful friend! Marcie joyfully said as she herself began to take off her own boots, and began to undress.

"I'll shower first!" The brunette said as she headed towards the bathroom"

"Make it quick, gorgeous! We've got some gals to entertain!" Lucille said through laughter. Realizing how long it'd been since she felt this happy about doing ANYTHING.

"I'll make it quick because we have some FOOD to entertain, you crazy redhead! I am STARVING!" Marcie said as she turned on the shower, and stepped in.

After Marcie was done in the bathroom, and Lucy had taken her turn in the shower, both girls towel dried their hair and swept each other's locks up into beautiful braids that cascaded down each woman's breasts, and began deciding what to wear for the evening.

Lucy, suddenly remembering that Max probably need his makeshift litter box cleaned, quickly gathered it up, and walked out onto the porch, tossed the litter into a garbage bag she'd grabbed from the bathroom, tied it up tight so it wouldn't stink, and walked it over to the garbage cans behind the bunkhouses. Tossing it in and closing the lid, Lucy made her way back to her room.

"You're not ready yet, Red?" She suddenly heard Green yell from the dirt parking lot. Looking out behind her she watched him turn his back and head towards the kitchen doors that would take him to the dining hall.

"I'm gettin' there, Green!" She said as she stepped up onto the small porch and opened her door.

Just as she was closing the door to her bunkhouse behind her, she heard Julie and Trish walk out onto their small area of the porch, and begin discussing the breakfast ride that was on the schedule for the next morning. Lucille felt butterflies in her stomach, remembering the last time she had experienced the morning breakfast ride. She recalled the way her heart sunk as she photographed the morning, knowing it would be her last full day on the ranch she had fallen in love with the first time she ever stepped foot on it.

The memory of the way Green watched her that day, like a hawk on prey, was etched forever into her soul.

Before she let her mind carry her too much further into the past, she quickly dabbed a bit more of the neutral lipstick across her lips, and switched her dusty jeans and t-shirt that lay in a lump on the bunkhouse floor, for a simple light pink western broom skirt, a white Dolce and Gabbana tank top, a chunky turquoise necklace and earrings and a Navajo bracelet. She completed the quick ensemble with a silver Native American Concho belt, and a tan pair of Tony Lama boots, fresh out of the box, thanking Marcie in the back of her mind, for packing for her.

After a quick look in the mirror, and the thrill of approval she seldom allowed herself, she told Marcie she would meet her on the porch.

"That sounds great, my dear!" Marcie yelled from the bathroom as she finished putting on her own finishing touches, wearing a below the ankle length long jean skirt, red button up blouse with a deep neckline, turquoise and red jewelry and a pair of black boots.

Lucille opened the door, walked out onto the porch, and ran smack dab into the chest of Ray.

"Well hey there, pretty woman " Ray said as he steadied both of them by holding onto Lucille's shoulders. "Let's have a look at you, young lady."

Lucille blushed and then smiled. Ray stood back from her, and with a wink of approval that reminded her of her own father's gestures, said "Someone's having a change of heart, I see. It's good to see a twinkle in those pretty green eyes of yours, my friend."

Lucille beamed brightly up at Ray as he turned on one heel so that he was adjacent to the blushing redhead, and held out his elbow.

"Well hang on one second, Sir" Lucy quickly said as she opened the door to her room and yelled to Marcie that Ray was taking her to the dining hall. "Sounds good to me!" Marcie yelled back as Lucy shut the door.

Unable to suppress the smile that was spreading across her face, Lucy hooked her arm through Ray's, and happily allowed him to escort her across the lawn, and into the Dining House, where appetizer hour was just beginning.

Before he let Lucille slip over to a seat in between Julie and Trish, Ray said "Don't forget your camera at breakfast tomorrow, young lady. I'm officially commissioning you to create a documentary of the event, and you will be paid." And with that, Ray turned off towards the kitchen.

After saluting Ray with eager acceptance of her new role, she grabbed her seat between the two ladies, smiled at Deb who was seated across from her, planted a solid kiss on the cheek of Julie, winked at Trish, and gave a quick hello to the other ladies surrounding the table.

"I'm starving ladies, where are those appetizers I keep hearing about?" Lucille exclaimed to the ladies.

As if on cue, Matilda, looking radiant in a red suede western skirt and jacket, came in with Ray following behind her, both carrying a tray each of everything from bacon-wrapped shrimp, and Thai-fried duck wings, to artichoke dip and Indian flat bread.

"Dig in cowgirls" Matilda said with a smile as she and Ray set each tray down in the center of the long, wide harvest table.

Marcie entered the room, greeting everyone with a wide smile, bantering back forth with everyone about being a little bit late, then seated herself in an empty overstuffed chair across from Lucy.

"Ahhhh" Marcie said as she relaxed down into the insanely comfortable chair. "Where IS that Concierge?" She said to no one in particular.

At that moment, Ray scooted back to the kitchen and re-entered the dining area with a tray that had a dozen or more long stemmed, wide mouth glasses filled to the rim with what looked (and smelled) like a nicely chilled, buttery Chardonnay.

Lucille's salivary glands kicked in to overdrive at the precise moment that Marcie reached up and grabbed a wayward glass out of Ray's hand, that was headed right towards Lucy's outstretched hand.

"I'll take that one, thank you very much, Sir" the brunette said with a tooth filled Cheshire Cat grin. "And Miss Lucy will have an ice cold Iced Tea with a giant slab of lime if you don't mind."

Ray looked from one woman to the other, as Lucille kicked her best friend under the table, shrugged his shoulders and retreated back to the kitchen, returning shortly with another long stemmed glass, filled with iced tea and completed with a big slice of lime festively perched on the rim. Lucille gladly accepted the drink, clinked glasses with Marcie, mouthed the words "Thank You" to the smiling brunette, took a long cold drink of the refreshing iced tea, leaned back in her chair, and proceeded to join in the conversation with the most wonderful group of easy going gals she had ever had the pleasure of meeting.

She was so enthused with everyone's interactions with each-other, that she barely had time to think of Green, other than noticing that neither he, nor Terry, had shown up for Appetizers. Come to think of it, (she thought to herself,) neither had Sam.

Just then all three walked into the room looking like three cats that ate three canaries.

"Alright ladies, lets wrap it up and head to the table, supper's a waitin'" Terry said as he winked over at the bewildered Marcie, and equally bewildered Lucy.

The Kitchen Girls; the young ladies that normally tended to the Dining House and Kitchen, came in to clean up the appetizers and wine glasses, then hurried the ladies over towards the table.

Once everyone was seated around the harvest table, Sam and her crew of waitresses began serving up a fabulous supper of Roasted Prime Rib, Bacon-wrapped Asparagus with Feta topping, Garlic Mashed Potatoes, and a Cranberry Arugula Salad.

Most of the ladies began sampling a Carafe of Merlot that Matilda was passing around, but Marcie and Lucy both opted for Iced tea with a wedge of lime. Marcie knew that Lucille could smell the fragrant purple-colored wine from a mile away, so when the Carafe made its way to their side of the table, Marcie made sure to reach around behind Lucille and pass it to the waiting (and knowing) hands of Trish. Lucille was thankful for the gesture, as it certainly wouldn't have taken much for her to partake in a glass, and she knew she wouldn't/couldn't/probably didn't want to stop at just one.

Dinner conversation centered around tomorrow's early morning ride, and the Chuck wagon style breakfast that Lucille knew from her previous visit, was sure to be a huge hit.

Terry and Green showed back up just as the ladies were diving into the main course, grabbed a chair each at the end of the long table, nodded to all the gals, removed their cowboy hats, and dove into their own meals that were placed before them by two of the kitchen staff.

"Well ladies, I suspect each of you will be getting a good night's sleep tonight, we'll be up at sunrise for the breakfast ride in the morning." Terry said in between bites of the perfectly roasted prime rib. "All your horses will be saddled and ready to go, so we'll expect each of you to be at your respective horses by 6:00 a.m. sharp."

"So no bon fire under the stars tonight?" Trish asked innocently, as she rested her chin coyly in her folded hands and batted her eyelashes at Terry.

"Not tonight, Miss Trish" Terry laughed.

"But, who will sing us to sleep then?" the older woman continued. "I should think a strum or two of the guitar is in order, don't you ladies?" Trish looked around the table, winking with exaggeration at each of the women who were quickly nodding in, and voicing, their agreement. "

"Looks like you're on the Marquee for entertainment tonight" Green chimed in as he scooted back his chair, picked up his empty plate and headed into the kitchen, winking at Lucille as he walked by.

"Oh no you don't, HW"

Julie, who was sitting quietly at the end of the table, suddenly chimed in.

"Ray said earlier that where Terry goes, you go, and that's all there is to it."

Green flashed a grin at Julie, then looked over at Lucy who was smiling quietly at the camaraderie going on around her, and much to even Trish's surprise, he said "Only if it's the dancing kind of strumming, and only if I get the first dance with the prettiest lady at the table."

You could have heard a pin drop as Lucille looked right up into Green's eyes, and prayed to God that he was talking about her.

Before anyone could breathe a word, Green walked straight over to Lucille, took her by the hand, and lifted her right up out of her chair. Lucille stumbled as Green pulled her close to him, grinned a wide grin, and quickly waltzed her across the dining room floor, twirled her several times, and then seated her promptly back in her chair next to Marcie, whose jaw had dropped clear to the floor.

Trish, who was eating up the scenario before her like a kid at a Sea World show, squealed with delight and laughter as she clapped her hands, stomped her feet, and whistled.

"Wooooeeee Life is GRAND, ain't it!" she yelled as the whole lot of the western clad ladies whooped and hollered as well, in full agreement with the still cackling, effervescent older woman.

"Alright ladies, you win" Terry said as he excused himself from the table and headed to the door.

"Bonfire and geetar strummin' in 20, don't leave me waitin'."

With a wink and a nod made directly towards Marcie, he was out the door.

"Lucille!" Marcie whispered to her best friend. "That was AMAZING!" But Lucille didn't hear Marcie, she was too busy being overly concerned that a part of her heart, soul and mind was just exposed to every single person on the ranch, including Matilda and Ray; and she wasn't quite sure how she felt about that.

Marcie touched Lucille's wrist, shaking her from her thoughts.

"Honey, it's okay, it's okay, you didn't do anything wrong, sweetheart." Marcie whispered to her friend of 20+ years.

"I'm still married, Marcie..." Lucille whispered.

As the two sat there in quiet conversation, Trish took it upon herself to hurry everyone else out of the dining hall and towards the Bon Fire area.

After the last lady shut the door behind her, Marcie took a deep breath, muttered the words "no time like the present," and quietly said to her waiting friend: "Actually, Lucille... according to the public notices in your newspaper back home, you're about five days away from a thirty day absolute GODSEND."

"I'm WHAT???" Lucille said in a bewildered tone.

"You're..." and just before Marcie could finish, Terry poked his head back through the door, and in his best British accent said, "Scarlett darling, that wink was a hint for you to follow me."

Marcie jumped up, kissed her friend on the cheek and said, "I'll explain later!"

"You'll WHAT???" Lucille seethed.

But Marcie just up and ran out the door after Terry, leaving Lucille sitting and wondering just what the hell that statement was all about.

Chapter 11

Lucille sat in the dining hall for a good ten minutes before she reminded herself that everything was always a mystery when it came to her feelings for Hank, therefore Marcie's off handed comment probably didn't warrant her spending one more minute pondering over it.

She couldn't help but wonder, though, if the Public Notice was about a thirty day divorce. She'd often thought about that herself, but always chickened out, pretending beyond hope that her marriage to such an asshole, would get better.

"Hank doesn't have the balls to file for divorce." Lucille said out loud to the empty room.

The only person that would ever even THINK of letting Lucille get out of this horrific marriage she stupidly hung onto for the sake of sanctity, was she herself.

Hank wouldn't dream of initiating that which would most assuredly set her free from the abusive, manipulative, hateful chains that bound her. At least, she was pretty sure he wouldn't. He couldn't stand to be alone. She learned over the years that Hank liked being married for the status, because he thought it made him look good, and that was about it. He'd have to have another victim in the wings to take the leap of filing for divorce, first …. And though there had been plenty of red flags that Hank wasn't entirely faithful to her, she never had any concrete evidence. Except for the night that the Cedar Fire ripped through her California town — but that was too much for her to recall, so like always, she shut down her thoughts.

Rather than let her evening be ruined over something she wasn't even sure of, she decided she could either sit there in the empty dining room, and sulk until bedtime; or go down to the bon fire and join that crazy group of ladies she'd grown to adore in such a short time.

She chose the bon fire, and with that decision firmly made, she grabbed what was left of her iced tea, stood up, and headed out the door.

"Hey, Red!" Deb, the grey haired but younger woman who was normally quite soft spoken, yelled. "We thought you'd never show up!" she continued as she smiled widely at the approaching redhead, and made a patting motion on the log she was sitting on, signaling Lucille to have a seat on the space next to her.

Lucille readily accepted, and before she knew it she was singing along with the other ladies, whose smiling faces and twinkling eyes were awash in the glow of the fire, as Terry strummed his guitar, and quietly sang "Rocky Mountain High."

Most of the women sang along to the well known John Denver song, except for Julie, of course, who had not a single clue who the gone but not forgotten 70's music icon was. She made a concerted effort to join in the singing anyway.

"Well at least I've got the chorus part down!" Julie yelled out in the middle of the song.

Everyone laughed and giggled at the wonderful blonde headed youngest of the group. The kind of laughter that made one feel very much included, and loved.

And Julie felt exactly that way around this bunch.

As blonde as Julie was, she had an uncanny sense of intuition, and she sensed that Lucille had a story to tell, and could feel that it was only a matter of time before the green eyed redhead started down the road of a new life.

Although nobody in the group knew it, Julie was actually on a new road, herself. For the first time in a long time, she felt like she was a part of something, instead of the insecure wall flower that was constantly poked fun of, on her previous path.

Julie was blonde, there was no denying that, and there were countless moments when she didn't quite catch onto something fast enough. Some called it a flaw, and Julie knew it in the way her so called friends would treat her back home. But here, she felt like a comedian; the person she was deep down inside was actually a funny, lighthearted, and quite intelligent young woman.

Everyone here seemed to either help her over her inability to catch on fast enough, or they'd see right through some of her "I'm just pretending to be blonde moments" and laugh uproariously with her, at her intentionally funny antics. She felt more included, and more understood here than she ever had anywhere else in her life, and she made a mental note to remember that these were the types of friends she wanted to surround herself with when she landed on the spot of her new home, and her new life. Both of which she was headed to, after the last day on the dude ranch.

But that story is for another time. Julie was already on her new road in life, and she didn't need to tell her story just yet, especially while Lucille was just starting out on hers.

Lucille could see the wheels spinning in Julie's head as she glanced up at the pretty blonde from across the fire. She felt a kindred connection as Julie made eye contact with her, and held it as the two of them smiled at each other from across the distance. It was as if a magnetic field was somehow delivering familiar feelings back and forth between them, and Lucille had a good feeling that Julie was somehow aware that she was going through some interesting times.

The two held a knowing smile for a moment before continuing on with the singing and laughter that was surrounding the night.

Deb nudged Lucille in the side, and nodded her head towards an approaching figure. As Lucille looked up she could barely make out the shadowy figure of Green.

"I do believe he's coming for you, my friend" Deb whispered excitedly.

"Oh really, Deb?" Lucille asked Deb through a knowing smile. "And what makes you think he's coming for me?" she said.

"Oh honey, it's clear he's smitten on you, I see the way he looks at you, and I see the way you try not to look at him." Deb said through light laughter.

"Now Deb, you don't know me well enough to make such a comment, even though I know you mean well" Lucille replied through a giggle, hugging the woman in an endearing squeeze.

But Deb saw the twinkle in Lucille's eyes and she decided that she did in fact, at least know a smitten heart when she saw one.

"… and besides" Lucille continued as she held up her left hand and pointed to her ring finger. "I'm married."

"Are you?" Deb asked, looking straight into Lucille's eyes.

Before Lucille could get over the sudden feeling of having to explain herself, Terry switched gears away from another John Denver song, and began strumming good ol' Hank Sr.'s "Hey Good Lookin'."

That's when Green stepped around the open flames, made a straight line for Lucille, took her by the hand and led her over to an open space next to the fire, that allowed just enough room for dancing.

"Two step, with me, Red?" Green inquired as his lips smiled beneath his mustache, and his eyes twinkled in the firelight.

"Well no I... I don't know how" Lucille stammered.

"DON'T KNOW HOW TO TWO STEP?" Marcie yelled from the log she was perfectly situated on next to Terry. "Ha! Come on Lucille, you won several two step championships in your younger years, quit beating around the bush, and DANCE, WOMAN!"

At that moment, Green spun her around like a dancer atop a jewelry box, and just as she came to rest in Green's arms, her instincts kicked in, and with perfect rhythm she began two stepping with Green around the fire.

Lucille hadn't two-stepped in only God knows how long, and whether she was alright with it or not, didn't matter for once; she was having a ball, and the smile on her face showed it.

Green threw in every move he could think of, and Lucille happily moved right along with him.

Not even the sight of Terry playing the guitar could pull Marcie's eyes off the smiling face of her best friend, as the man who might very well be the one to save her life, twirled Lucille around the dirt desert floor.

When Terry strummed the last string of "How's about cookin' somethin' up with me" Green tilted Lucille so far back that the curls at the end of her loose braid, touched the dirt.

All the ladies whooped, hollered and clapped as Green and Lucille maintained their stance. Both began to laugh while they worked to catch their breath after the fast dance, as Green lifted Lucille back up to a standing position, they both bowed to the crowd around them. Ray and Matilda clapped the loudest, and as Terry strummed another tune, Ray grabbed Matilda's arm and began to twirl his smiling wife of 53 years, around the light of the bon fire.

Marcie moved closer to Terry, and was rewarded by a wink and a smile from the strumming cowboy. As she looked around at all the smiling faces of the women she was spending this eye-opening week with, she felt that all was completely right with the world.

"Well move over, Marcie, and grab that geetar!" Trish said as she jumped up off the log she had been sitting on. "A little bird told me you could really strum, and I'd like a chance at a dance with this tall drink of water of yours!" she continued, her eyes twinkling with mischief and laughter.

Marcie knew she wouldn't get out of this one, and as she gently took over the guitar from Terry, she heard him say to Trish "Alright, there fair lady, but just keep in mind that I'm already taken, so don't get any strange ideas in that pretty head of yours!" Trish just laughed knowingly.

When Terry swung her around, so his back was to Marcie, Trish peeked up over Terry's shoulder and gave Marcie the biggest, most exaggerative wink a gal could give, and yelled "Play it Sam!"

Without skipping a beat, Marcie (much to everyone's utter surprise) broke into the wildest guitar version of "Chatahoochie" the world had ever heard.

As the night grew on, and Ray and Matilda bid their goodnights to everyone, Terry waltzed Trish back over to her respective log, and made stride back to the still strumming Marcie. Lifting her up off her seated position he handed the guitar off to Trish, who cackled and said aloud "I can't play this thing" to which Terry responded with "We'll make our own music, Miss Trish," and with a twist of his arm he twirled Marcie around the fire until both of them were completely out of breath.

Green and Lucille were sitting together after their two stepping dance moves, watching the events of what was left of the night play out, being careful not to touch, though the fire between them was burning hotter than the fire in front of them.

Lucille simply could not put herself in another "guilt-ridden" position, and Green was in no hurry to disrespect her unspoken wishes.

"Dancing is one thing" Lucille said to herself rather matter of factly. "Touching hands in front of everyone, is a hole 'nother ball game." Aside from that, Lucille felt she'd done too much already anyway. Deciding to keep on enjoying herself, she joined in the singing with the others.

Green was intently watching her, marveling at the way she was smiling and singing along with everyone. He really hadn't seen her relaxed at all in her previous visit, and he decided that the priceless look of happiness and ease on her face, was far worth knowing that he was going to have to wait until this woman he had fallen in love with, was ready to make the change that would let him in.

"Oh Best Friend O' Mine!" Marcie yelled across the fire to Lucy as Terry swung her one last turn and sat her down on a log. "Would you come sit a spell with me, pretty please!" She continued as she batted her eyelashes, and patted the log beside her.

Lucy gave a quick smile to Green and stood up, who in turn gave her a wink back, and made her way around the flames and over to Marcie where she seated herself down on the log that Marcie was still patting.

The two began a quiet discussion that seemed to blanket the evening with that old familiar "The party's over" feeling, and one by one the ladies downed the last of their drinks.

Julie, Deb and Trish all stood up at the same time as the other ladies did, bid their goodnights to each other and to Green, Lucille, Terry and Marcie, and headed to their bunk houses to turn in for the night.

"See you at the corrals in the morning, Cowgirls!" Lucille yelled off to the retreating ladies. "Race you to 'em at first light, Trish!" She continued loudly, to which the happy older gal responded in the way she was quickly becoming known for; one arm straight up in the air, middle finger a flyin'.

"You bet your sweet ass I will, Red!" Trish cackled as she made her way to her own bunkhouse room.

As the laughter dwindled away into the distance, both men looked at the two women sitting beside each other in front of the bon fire. They had returned to what looked like a very deep conversation.

"Reckon we should leave those two alone, Old Man?" Green said to Terry.

"Reckon that's a good idea, Green. Looks to me like they've got some soul searching going on." Terry responded.

"Don't we all, Old Man... Don't we all" Green said quietly as he continued watching the two ladies lost in conversation.

Terry walked over to Marcie with the intention of saying goodnight, but Marcie stood up and looked right into Terry's eyes. Tipping his hat, he bid adieu to her, and in response Marcie leaned forward on her tip toes and planted a kiss right on the unsuspecting cowboy's lips. Knowing that all the other ladies, and Ray and Matilda had since long gone, Terry wrapped the brunette up in his arms and returned the favor with a long and gentle kiss. When he finally released her he looked deep into her eyes and whispered "You're going to be mine before this trip is over, Marcie." To which Marcie responded with a wink, "I guess that will depend on how good breakfast is, Terry."

Before Terry could respond, Green interrupted and said that he was heading in for the night too, and would walk both girls back to their bunkhouse. In response, Marcie suddenly remembered that she had left something in the dining house, and quickly retreated before Lucille could contest. Terry was quick to follow the quickly exiting brunette.

"Night Miss Lucy" Terry said as he tipped his hat to her and skirted on after Marcie.

"G'night, Green!" Lucy yelled after the tall cowboy chasing her best friend.

"Yeah, that's "Terry," Miss Lucy; I'm "Green" the Head Wrangler said, using two fingers on each hand to indicate quotes as he mentioned Terry's name, and then his.

"Oh!" Lucille laughed aloud "Oh how funny," she exclaimed, as she felt her ears begin to burn with embarrassment.

"You either have that color on your mind, or you can't stop thinking of me." Green said as he looked deep into her eyes.

"Both" Lucille whispered as Green took a seat beside her, and the smoldering heartfelt tension between them grew.

"That's what I thought" Green whispered. His face so close to hers she thought she might pass out from the feelings welling up inside her.

For a moment they just stared at each other. Heart beats quickening in the night that surrounded them.

"You'd better go put that fire out, Cowboy, and walk me back to my room before the sun comes up." Lucille said as she broke the silence between them.

"I really don't want to put this fire out, Lucille" Green said. "Do you?"

"I can't answer that right now, Green." Lucille responded quietly. "I hope you can somehow understand that."

"I know about your husband, Lucille" and before she could stop him he continued.

97

"I know about how he treated you, still treats you, and I know about your drinking" Green quietly said to Lucille as he watched her head lower in shame.

"Please don't be embarrassed, Lucy" he said as he lifted her chin up, and looked into her eyes.

"I'll wait for you to do whatever it is you need to do, in your own time, but I'll wait for you, Lucy. I'll wait for you because I love you, and I want to take you back to Wyoming with me when my term here is up, but I'll always wait for you." Green continued.

"And what if I can't make a change, Green?" Lucille quietly said. "What if I go back two days from now, and I can't make any change? What will you do then, Green? Will you stay here waiting for me, knowing even then, that you might be waiting forever?" Lucille looked away from Green's eyes, as she continued.

"You don't want a woman like me, Cowboy... you don't want or need the baggage that comes with a woman who has allowed herself years of abuse, and who drinks like a fish so that she can pretend her life is perfect."

Tears began to quietly stream down Lucille's face as she looked at him and said, "I Love you, Green, God forgive me, I love you, but there isn't anything I can do about that right now, and I don't know if there will ever be anything I can do about it."

Green just stared in wonder at the woman sitting next to him.

"What kind of idiot lets a woman like you go, Lucille?" Green said as he traced his hand along her cheekbone, gently wiping away the tears that were now falling from her eyes.

"What kind of monster must he be, not to see the woman he has in you?"

A lengthy quiet fell between them, and Lucille broke that silence by moving away from this man she could no longer deny loving.

Standing up she looked down at him and said "Green, I better get back to the bunkhouse now, that Arizona sun will come up early tomorrow morning, and I don't want to be in bad shape for the Breakfast ride. Having said that, would you do me a favor and put me back in the great mood I was in before everyone left for bed? Because if you don't, I am going to cry myself to sleep, and nobody likes a baggy eyed cowgirl in the morning."

Green couldn't help but smile, and taking the cue to leave well enough alone, (for now,) grabbed Lucy by her right hand and swung her out into a fast spin over the lawn that separated the bunkhouses from the bonfire area, following with a two step along behind her as he spun her round and round.

Marveling at the beauty twirling so close to him, he didn't see the log that she had so elegantly jumped over until it was too late. Green tripped, stumbled and then crashed to the ground, making sure to bring Lucille down with him. Had it been any other moment, they both could have easily fallen into another round of unbridled passion, but Green maintained a light attitude and began laughing instead. He laughed so hard that he thought his gut would split, and as Lucille wiggled out from underneath him, she began to laugh as well.

"Not so light on your feet these days, eh old man?" Lucille giggled as she spoke. "I think that did the trick, Green, you made me laugh again, so you go on and make sure that bon fire is out, and I'll make my way back to my room by myself."

Before Green could argue (or stand up) Lucille was moving off at a fast pace towards the bunk houses, and Green could hear her giggling as she faded off into the distance.

"You better not let that one get away again" Green heard a soft voice say in the dark. He turned towards the voice and watched Marcie enter what was left of the light from the bonfire.

"Don't reckon that I want to, Miss Marcie, but don't reckon that I have that choice at the moment, now do I?" He asked her.

"Actually, Green" Marcie quietly and with great intention, whispered "You just might." She said as she handed Green a yellow envelope addressed to Marcie Noland, c/o the Dusty Bar Trails Ranch in Wickenburg, Arizona.

Green grabbed the envelope and stood up. "What's this about, Marcie?"

"It's a Newspaper from San Diego County, Green. It's the Public Notices section. Take it back to your bunk house and read it, I need to go talk to Lucy."

Without so much as another word, she headed off into the direction of her room, and her best friend.

Green was silent as he pondered reading what was in his hands right now, versus waiting until he arrived back at his bunk; realizing the light from the fire was almost completely out now, without his reading glasses (that he couldn't find,) he was almost as blind as a bat when it came to reading fine print. Green shook his head in wonder, pocketed the yellow envelope, put out the remaining coals, and headed off in the opposite direction of the girl's bunkhouses, to his own quarters that he shared with Terry; a cowboy he had known and worked with on this very ranch for almost seven of the fifteen years that Terry had wrangled here. A Cowboy that he trusted dearly.

Opening the door to his quarters, he saw Terry sitting in a lay-z-boy in front of a small fire in the fireplace. October Arizona nights could sometimes get a little cool, and with no temperature controls in their cabin, Terry had lighted a small fire to take the edge off. With a wave of his arm, he motioned Green to sit down.

Realizing the clock said only 9:30pm, Green decided he had enough time to join him for a spell.

"Marcie give you an envelope, Green?" Terry said without looking up from the magazine he was reading.

"She sure did, Old Man." Green responded.

"d'you read what was inside, yet?"
"Nope, too dark and I can't read without my glasses" Green said.

Terry, without looking up, held up his hand, showing a pair of reading glasses, and motioning them towards Green.

Green just grinned and shook his head, never ceasing to be amazed at how well his friend knew him.

"Well alright then, Terry" Green said as he grabbed the glasses from his friend's hand, and put them on.

"Let's see what the sudden fuss is all about," he said as he sat down in the lay-z-boy that sat opposite Terry's, still in front of the fire.

Green studied the front of the large yellow envelope, reading aloud the address, and to whom it was addressed to.

"Now why do you 'spose Marcie would want me to read something addressed to her, Terry?" Green said as he tapped the yellow envelope on his knee.

"Because it's not about Marcie, Old Boy." Terry said matter of factly as he flipped a page over in his magazine.

"It's about Lucy ..." Terry continued as he flipped another page.

Green froze for a moment.

"What did a newspaper of Pubic Notices have to do with Lucy?" Green thought to himself.

"Go on now, open it, read it, and get it over with." Terry said. "Sunrise comes early, and we'll have much to talk about before then, Green"

Without further hesitation, Green pulled the newspaper out of the envelope, and scanned the Public Notices before him, stopping when he saw the name of the woman he loved, in the second notice of the "Notice of Divorce" section.

"Terry, this says ..."

Before Green could complete his sentence, Terry said "I know what it says, Green; now what are you going to do about it?" He continued, closing the magazine, and looking right at his friend.

...the two men talked into the night, finally turning in as the chimes struck 2:00 a.m. on the old grandfather clock Green brought with him, when he first checked into the ranch some seven years ago.

Green fell fast asleep with dreams of a new future at the forefront of his mind.

Terry fell fast asleep with dreams of a beautiful, vivacious brunette named 'Marcie,' at the forefront of his mind.

Neither of the two men slept very fitfully.

Chapter 12

Marcie yawned and slowly opened her eyes as the 5am alarm went off on the nightstand beside her. Something furry was laying on her arm, which was numb from the weight of what she now realized was Max; Lucy's faithful cat.

"Oh Max, what are you doing over here?" She said to the yawning Maincoon. Max arched his back in response, hopped down off the bed, and made his way to the litter box in the bathroom.

"You're practically human, you know that, fat cat?" Marcie said, as she propped herself up on one elbow, and turned on the bedside lamp beside her.

The first thing Marcie noticed as the light of the morning began to spread across the room, was that Lucille was not in her bed. She knew she wasn't in the bathroom, because the lights were off.

Aww shit, Marcie said aloud as she swung her legs over the side of the bed, stretched her back and rubbed her eyes.

Marcie's intention when she got back to the bunkhouse last night, was to talk to her Lucy about the piece of mail that Matilda had slipped to Marcie at the bonfire while Green and Lucy were dancing. But Lucy was fast asleep when she walked in after her own late night with Terry, and Marcie didn't have the heart to wake her. Now with worry on her mind, she wished she had. Lucy was known to bolt when things got confusing … and though Marcie told herself she wouldn't be mad if she did bolt, she also told herself she would be super mad if her best friend bolted in her beloved pickup truck.

Opting not to shower, Marcie quickly dressed in a fresh pair of jeans, her black cowboy boots, and a blue, ribbed, long tail tank top. Twisting her dark locks up into a loose bun, securely set in place with the pull of a hair band, Marcie applied a quick dab of lipstick, donned her Prada sunglasses, and made a beeline for the corrals as the early morning sun began to rise over the ranch.

Just as she thought, Lucy was there, seated on the ground and leaning up against a watering trough.

"Good thing I hid the spare keys to my truck, my friend" Marcie said as she seated herself onto the dusty ground next to Lucille.

"Good thing Max didn't want to go with me, or I'd of used the key that's still in your ignition." Lucille said as she drew a few circles in the dirt with a stone she was piddling with.

"That fat cat knows you best, Lucy." Marcie said as she smiled at her best friend.

"Speaking of ... Cat got your tongue?"

"No Marce, I guess I just need some quiet time, if you don't mind?" She said as she reached over and squeezed her knee and said, "you and I are fine, please don't take this personally."

"Ok honey," Marcie conceded. Not that she wanted to, but she realized that talking with Lucille about anything right now, before the breakfast ride, would screw up her best friend's chances of photographing the would be moment creatively, and from the heart.

Marcie hoisted herself off the ground, dusted off her back side, bent over and kissed her friend on the top of her head, and walked over to the tack room where she could see a shadow of a movement inside.

"Ah Hoy!" Marcie said as she walked into the dimly lit room.

"Well hey there beautiful" Terry said as he turned towards Marcie. His eyes looking her up and down, taking in the beauty standing in front of him.

"Ready for breakfast, Miss Scarlett?"

"I sure am, Rhett" she said in return to the low and sexy voice coming from Terry, as he slow approached her, wrapped his arms around her and pulled her to him.

"You are a sight for sore eyes" the tall cowboy said as he leaned in and kissed Marcie gently on the lips.

"Good morning" he said in the sexiest tone her insides had ever heard.

"Good morning to you" Marcie said in return as she leaned in closer to Terry, pressing her lips to his in a fiery display of passion.

Terry pulled away slowly and looked deep into the eyes of the woman he could not deny falling in love with.

"Up to helping this old hand ready some horses for this breakfast ride, mi lady?"

"Just show me the ropes." Marcie replied.

Terry led her over to where the feed sacks were already filled and ready to go, showed her where the name was on each bag indicating which horse gets which bag, and sent her off into the corrals with an armful, where she set out hanging one across the head of each horse, all of which were more than happy to oblige her.

She was a natural around horses, and always seemed to pick up quickly the tasks set before her when it pertained to them. Even if she'd never really been completely as engrossed as Lucille was in the knowledge of these beautiful creatures, she was still a pretty solid horsewoman, if she did say so herself.

As the sun came up higher over the corrals, all the ladies began arriving one by one, bright eyed and bushy tailed, just as Marcie was finishing up hanging the last bag around the ears of her own horse for the week "Diamond Ring."

"Well haaaayyy" Julie said in a sweet but comical voice as she walked up to Marcie and hugged her good morning.

"Hay is for horses" Marcie said laughingly as she returned the friendly squeeze.

"Guuurrrrllll, I am sooooooooooo like SOOOOOOOOO totally ready for this ride" Julie said as she walked over to "Moonshine" the tall Palomino mare that was designated to her for the week, and began showering the horse with kisses.

Terry came back out just as Julie was patting down the neck of the beautiful gelding, and instructed all the ladies to brush out their horses while they finished their breakfast of grains, and then to remove their respective feedbags when they were done.

Lucille had already stood up from her thinking position on the ground just moments before the first few ladies trickled in, and was concentrating on a few burrs that were stuck in Lucky's mane. Each lady said a lovingly and very genuine good morning to the redhead, and Lucy was thankful for their intuition in knowing that she needed some head space.

As she was checking her camera gear, and loading the saddle bags with what lenses she knew she would need; Green, who had just walked into the corrals after a coffee meeting with Ray and Matilda, placed his hands on Lucy's shoulders and turned her towards him.

"Good morning, Miss Lucy" Green said as he reached up and brushed a line of hair away from her porcelain face.

"Good morning to you, Green" she responded with a wide smile.

Happy to see him, and relieved at the stress in her shoulders that suddenly left her body at Green's touch, she realized that this man before her had an uncanny way of making her feel both at ease, and (odd as it may sound) adequate. Two things Hank was good at in the beginning of their relationship but stole from her not long after they were married, ensuring her with every chance he got, that she was far from worthy of, or any good at, much of anything, especially horses.

Out of respect for the rest of the ladies, and his job in general as Head Wrangler on the Dusty Bar Trails, Green held himself back from kissing the beauty before him, and instead squeezed her shoulder and said, "Got those special tools ready that you'll need for the extraordinary images I know you'll capture, Lucy?"

"Ready and waiting, Cowboy" Lucy said with a smile. Grateful for the encouraging words that rang in her ears.

"Well let's saddle up." Green said, as he smiled at her beneath his mustache.

"We'll need to get going so you can snap a few shots of the gals riding into the breakfast area on their horses.   There's lots of Saguaro Cactus along the way, and Matilda says she'd love some shots of horseback riders beneath them." He said as Lucy buckled up the last saddle bag.

Remembering how tall some of the Saguaro were along the way to the breakfast ride last year, Lucy readily agreed, checked her stirrups, exchanged Lucky's halter for his bridle, and hoisted herself up into the saddle; excited at the prospect of creating some good marketing materials for the ranch she had grown to love, as well as the dawned awareness that Green said the words "we'll need to get going," which meant she'd be riding alone with the man who was quickly overtaking a heart that she thought was long dead and void of any real feelings.

Green, who'd already saddled up his mare at dusk after feeding her an early breakfast of grains and alfalfa, placed one foot in the stirrup and with the ease of a cowboy who knew no other life but being in the saddle, swung his leg up and over his horse, and seated himself comfortably.

Reaching down to release the "git-down" rope that he preferred in place of a tie, he wrapped the rope and tied it securely with saddle strings, to the front of his saddle. With a few clicks and easy turn of his horse with the reins, he motioned Lucille to follow along as he made his way towards the opening of the corrals.

As if Lucky knew the adventure they were heading out on, the old horse took the lead from his faithful rider, and without so much as a nudge from Lucy, turned and followed Green.

Like clockwork Lucy watched Green reach up and touch the now familiar sign with his fingertips, to which she followed suit, and the two of them picked up the pace as they rode out over Wickenburg's desert floor. Green took her up high so that Lucy could overlook a draw that Terry would be bringing the girls through on their horses.

"And so we wait, beautiful" Green said as he stopped his horse and turned in his saddle towards her.

"And so we do!" Lucy responded excitedly, surprised by the elevated tone of excitement coming from her own voice after such an emotional morning. Although readying herself for any photo shoot could bring her out of just about any bad mood, no matter what she was photographing. She loved the camera, as well as the images she was blessed enough to be able to capture throughout her life as a career photographer.

Settling in on her saddle, and looking out over the draw below, Lucille quietly realized that Green had taken her and the group she was riding with, up on this exact same ridge of the Bradshaw Mountains, the first time she rode on the Dusty Bar Trails Ranch a little over a year ago.

Only that time she was absolutely terrified to walk her horse across that ridge, and since Lucky could sense her fear, he wasn't having any of it either.

Before she could stop it, the memory of that rainy late afternoon a year ago, came washing over her.

"Something wrong, Red?" Green said to her as she kept her horse at a still while the other riders passed on by Green, confidently walking their horses atop one of the high ridges of the Bradshaw Mountains, just up from the ranch.

106

"I really can't go over that Green, I'm just going to turn my horse around and head back to the ranch."

"Lucky doesn't know how to get back to the ranch on his own." Green said through a smile that made the laugh lines on the sides of his eyes evident even underneath the shadow of his hat.

"Yes he does, Green" Lucy said impatiently.

"Nope, he's dumb as a rock when it comes to knowing how to go back home, you'll be stuck out here forever if you don't let him walk you across that ridge, Lucy."

"Green, Lucky is the smartest horse I know, now go on with the others, I'll see you back at the ranch."

"Suit yerself, Red" Green said as he turned his horse to the group ahead.

As soon as Green was a little ways ahead, Lucy took her reigns and turned Lucky back towards the ranch. With a few clicks of her tongue and a squeeze of her heels, Lucy readied herself for the ride back.

Lucky didn't move an inch.

With a few more clicks of her tongue and a squeeze of her heels, Lucy once again readied herself for the ride back.

Lucky still didn't move an inch.

Frustrated, Lucy turned Lucky back in the direction of the group, and Lucky began to move forward, so Lucy took the opportunity of movement, to head him back to the ranch.

Lucky turned back towards the ranch, and then planted his feet firmly, standing stock still.

"Oh come on honey" Lucy said to the horse she was completely smitten with. "I can't ride across that ridge, it brings back too many bad memories, Lucky… memories that scare the living shit out of me, and memories that I really don't need a reason to re-live."

Lucky moved his ears back and forth, listening to his rider as she spoke.

And still he remained — stock still.

107

Lucy gave a few kicks of her heels into the flanks of Lucky's sides and made fast forward moving movements in the saddle as if doing so would force the 1200lb animal to step ahead.

But he didn't.

Lucy, frustrated at her own fear, and her own awareness of not being half the rider she used to be before she broke her leg in half in a horse riding accident years ago, felt a lump in her throat form at the thought of having to cross that ridge.

It wasn't just the fear of the memory of the accident that caused tears to start flowing down her cheeks… it was the memories of the horrible marriage she was still stuck in, that came crashing to the forefront of her mind. It was the memories of the times Hank beat her, even while her leg was still in a cast. It was the memory that even while she lay below the ridge that she and her horse fell from, Hank was nowhere to be seen, just like always — he was never, ever, there for her.

She went through almost everything on her own, whether it was good or bad. And she never breathed a word to anyone about the abuse, except the police, when she begged them not to haul her husband away after the neighbors who lived behind called the police one night, when Hank had her in a choke hold in their backyard. It was the third time she bailed him out of jail. Even the death of her older sister was something she had to endure on her own, because jackass Hank insisted on going to a rodeo meeting in town, rather than sit with his wife, while her older sister took her last breaths after a short bout with Inflammatory Breast Cancer.

It was also the reality that she could no longer ride a horse with the kind of confidence that she used to have, even on a horse named Lucky. The reality that she really couldn't do very much of anything anymore without feeling some kind of fear, doubt or inadequacy; which is exactly why she took the job of photographing ranches for three months, to get away from Hank for awhile, in hopes he would start to miss her, in hopes that her marriage would resolve. And to see if she could find herself again, to see if she could find her way back to the vibrant, sober, intelligent, humorous, confidant woman she once was.

At the moment, she wasn't finding shit.

"Hey Red" a soft voice behind her, sounded.

Turning in her saddle she saw Green sitting atop his mare, staring intently at her.

108

"You came back" Lucille quietly said as she hurriedly wiped the tears from her face with the sleeve of her shirt.

"I realized it wasn't stubbornness that was keeping you from following along with us, Lucy." Green said as he dismounted and walked his horse over to where Lucy and Lucky were still standing… stock still.

"What made you realize that about me, Green?" Lucy said through a few sniffles.

"My Boss, Ray." Green responded as he stood beside Lucy and looked up at her sitting in the saddle.

"Your boss?"

"Yep. I radioed down to the corrals to ask Terry to come up here and get you so I didn't need to leave the group behind, but Ray answered." Green continued.

"He told me that you had some kind of accident awhile back, and that it was probably what was making you too scared to cross that ridge with me. So he sent Terry up the short route to pick up the head of the group on the ridge and sent me back for you."

"So you really were going to leave me out here by myself, Green?"

"I'm here now, aren't I, Red?" Green said.

Only he said it in such a way that Lucy, from atop her saddle, couldn't help but stare right down into Green's eyes, the bluest eyes she'd ever seen, as he looked right up into hers. For a moment the small space between them disappeared as Green continued to stare intently into the depths of Lucy's soul… a space suddenly replaced with the yearning tension that only two people about to fall in love, could feel. An indescribable feeling that Lucy could tell was generating a fast, thick current of electricity between them, and she found it hard to pull her eyes away from his.

Green spoke first, never taking his eyes off of her. "Lucy, do you want to tell me what happened?"

"Not really, Green."

"Do you want to to walk across that ridge, and put that fear behind you once and for all?" Green responded.

"I can't" Lucy whispered.

"You can, I'll be right here with you, you'll be safe with me, I promise."

Lucy couldn't help but let another tear slide out of her eye and down her nose, landing on her upper lip. Wiping the tear away with her hand she nodded her head and said "Okay, Green, I'll walk across that ridge with you."

"Green pulled his eyes away to make a quick check of Lucy's stirrup, and then walked around to check the other stirrup. He looked up at her again and said, "you believe me when I tell you you're safe with me, right, Red?"

"Yes, I ... I believe you." Lucy said. For a fleeting moment she doubted her safety and doubted her abilities; but she realized she didn't doubt him.

She also realized that he was quickly awakening within her, feelings she'd long given up on.

"Ready, beautiful?" Green said, startling Lucy away from her runaway brain. She didn't know how to respond to something she hadn't heard in years, but she knew it made her heart beat more wildly than she could control.

"I .. you called me beautiful, Green.."

"Because you are." Green said quietly.

"Turn Lucky towards me, give him his reign, and he will do the rest. You just enjoy the scenery for me, ok?" Green said.

"Okay, Green"

"You alright?" He asked the redhead sitting before him.

"I'm alright"

"You know you can do this, right?"

"Only because of you, Green."

"Naw Lucy, you just forgot what you're made of, you've got this, honey."

Lucy knew by the way Green was looking at her, that she had nothing to fear. And for once in about ten years, Lucy felt safe. Safe enough to take the chance that she could follow this cowboy across one of the highest ridges on the ranch, safe enough that the thought that she might fail in front of him, simply didn't cross her mind. Safe enough that the memories she was so afraid would surface ...

Didn't.

Green took the lead and moved his horse out on the ridge, turning back in his saddle to watch her ride behind him, giving his mare the reigns. Never taking his eyes off of her, she watched him as his body slowly rocked in the saddle to the walking rhythm of his horse. Their eyes were locked so intently, that Lucy caught herself imagining what it would be like to be underneath a man that moved like that. To be underneath THAT man, that moved like that.

Unable to control the fire that was building deep inside her, Lucy broke the silence between them as they continued their rhythmic dance across the ridge that was bathed in the golden light of Arizona's setting sun.

"What am I made of, Green?" Lucy said, barely audible through the musky feelings she was feeling as she spoke.

"Iron, and Steele and Roses, Lucy ... that's what you're made of, that's who you are, and that's who you need to get back to when you leave Wickenburg" Green said in a tone that made her wish she could succumb to the passion that was building inside her. A passion that he was building inside her.

Green turned back forward in his saddle as they crossed the last few feet of the ridge, heading back down to the desert floor, and Lucy let the words he said ring in her ears.

"Iron, and Steele and Roses, Lucy ... that's what you're made of, that's who you are, and that's who you need to get back to when you leave Wickenburg"

Lucy knew something changed for her up on that ridge. She wasn't quite sure what it was just yet, but she could feel a new season of life welling up inside her, and she hoped beyond hope that when she left Wickenburg tomorrow afternoon, that she wouldn't lose sight of the awareness creeping over her, that deep down she was still the same courageous horsewoman that she was before she married Hank.

Chapter 13

Jarring herself from yet another quick memory, she readied herself as Green pointed and explained to Lucille where Terry and the girls would start showing up, and which trail they'd be on, and which Saguaros they'd be closest to. Still shaking herself from the memory she had recalled, she twisted her telephoto super fast long lens on one Nikon body, and a short zoom lens on her second Nikon body. She placed both straps over her right shoulder, placed the body of the Nikon with the telephoto lens between her legs, and rested the front of the lens on the saddle horn, while the other camera rested on the thigh of her right leg.

Just as she recalled he would do, Lucky's ears went straight up and tipped as far forward as they could go, every few seconds rotating backwards waiting for her cue to step forward or whoa. She had never ridden a horse so camera ready - the memories of just how in-tune this horse was with her shooting, came flooding back to her as the first sign of the trail riders heading towards the Chuck Wagon Breakfast, began to creep around the Saguaros below.

"Better get that camera up, beautiful" Green said. Although it was the second time he'd called her "beautiful" in a matter of minutes, Lucy's heart fluttered just the same as the first time he said it.

"Yessir, HW" Lucy said as she lifted up the camera with the long lens to her eye, steadied her elbow on the saddle horn, and began shooting the beautiful scene unraveling below her.

"Nothing quite like cowboys and cowgirls on horseback weaving in and out of Saguaro, Green" Lucille said as she switched cameras to grab a panoramic shot of the group riding in single file amongst dozens of three and four and five armed Cacti.

"Nothing quite like watching the most beautiful lady in the world, doing what she loves most." Green said as he keenly watched her capturing the scene below.

He recalled the way he felt the first time he ever watched her shoot. She was photographing him, and he could feel her in his soul with each click of the camera. He had never felt so calm and confident in front of a lens before, as he did the first time he ever laid eyes on the photographer that he now hoped would soon be his.

"Let's move on up towards the breakfast site, Lucy." Green said as he turned his horse to head up to where Ray, Matilda and the girls were cooking up breakfast over an open fire in cast iron pots and pans. "Matilda wants some shots of them cooking, and the grub and all."

With one last click of the shutter, Lucille obliged, and while keeping both cameras at her side, her right arm through both straps like a sling to hold them steady, she moved Lucky towards Green, and the duo began the short hike up the rest of the foothill that would lead them to breakfast.

Upon arrival at the site, Ray and Matilda looked up from their respective positions of cooking eggs, bacon, sausage, biscuits and gravy over large open fires, and waved at the two of them as they rode up and dismounted. Sam the female wrangler, and another gal named Eileen came up and took both horses, and walked them over to the hookup line under a large Mesquite tree.

The smells of the breakfast combined with the smells of the open fires was a little more than Lucille could take as she realized just how hungry she was.

"Hey Red, Darlin!" Ray yelled over to Lucille.

"Come on over here and have a biscuit and coffee while we wait for the troop to show up"

Lucille smiled and headed over in the direction of the food and happily caught a tossed biscuit from Ray, and a cup of coffee in an old metal mug from Matilda.

"We're so happy to have you here with us again, Lucy. Matilda said. "No one captures the ambience of the ranch and our visitors, quite like you do" the older woman continued with a smile.

Matilda was a radiant woman, eclectically dressed even for a breakfast ride, that few could pull off like she did. Her smile lit up the entire desert and her eyes left nothing unsaid. She was a real cattle woman, the kind whose memory never leaves your mind.

Lucille caught herself wondering if the mere fact that she was married to Ray, kept her as young, confident and magnificent as she genuinely portrayed herself to be.

Recalling the first and only time she ever had the pleasure of riding with Matilda, Lucy had never seen a woman sit as comfortably in the saddle. In fact, she'd never really ever seen anyone, male or female, seat a horse quite like Matilda did. She was her favorite subject to photograph the first time Lucille came to the ranch, and her favorite photograph from that trip was a photo she had captured of the keeper of Ray's heart, sitting atop her horse overlooking a draw that crept across the Sonoran floor in twists and turns.

"I am so happy to be back, Miss Matilda" Lucy responded. "I ... I know, I mean I wish that I could have somehow let you all know that I was coming back, but it was something I just ... I really didn't have any control over, and I am so sorry if I caused any kind of misinterpretation of myself." Lucille said as she looked in the older woman's eyes.

"Lucy, we all have baggage that we don't like to talk about, you know." Said Matilda. "And sometimes we drag it behind us until we learn to put it down."

Lucille wasn't quite sure how to respond to such a profound statement, and so rather than search for words that weren't there, she simply reached out and wrapped both arms around the wise cattle-woman; a biscuit in one hand, and a cup of coffee in the other and simply said "Thank you."

As she pulled away from the quick embrace, she could hear the whoop and holler of the ladies coming around the bend towards camp. Getting down on one knee in her signature tripod position, she heard one voice in particular exclaim "Take THAT John Wayne" as a smiling and exuberant Trish trotted to a stop in front of Lucille, (who had begun busily photographing the moment,) and beamed down on her from atop the big draft that she was so excited to ride for the week.

"Oh Lucy, you missed out on theeee RiiiiDE of the CENTURY!" Trish said as she climbed down off of her horse, hanging for a minute before she let herself drop to both feet.

"Accckkkk!" Trish yelled — these girls were not made to slide down the side of a saddle!" she said as she adjusted her front side, and handed her reigns over to Sam. "Now where's that coffee I've been smellin' since we left the ranch?"

Lucy watched her new friend quickly short step over to Matilda who handed the woman a hot cup of coffee.

As Lucille stayed in her current position to photograph the rest of the gang coming in, Green reached out to her, grabbed one of her cameras off of her shoulders and said "I'll hold one until you need it,

Red" and with that, Lucy began shooting with her short lens, as one by one each woman slid to a stop, dismounted and handed their horses off to Sam and Eileen.

Just then, Terry rounded the corner, tall in the saddle wearing a navy blue silk scarf, a cream colored cowboy hat with brown trim, a Wrangler denim shirt and jeans, and chaps that had rivets all down the sides in a straight line that made his long legs look even longer than they already were.

Lucy could feel her heart race as she snapped pic after pic of the Cowboy as he pulled the big roan he was riding today, up to a stop in front of her. She could always feel when she was capturing an extraordinary moment. And it didn't get much more "Cowboy Extraordinary" than this.

"Go back and do that again, Terry" Lucy said.

Without even asking why, Terry turned his horse around and headed back into the brush that separated the breakfast site from the rest of the Sonoran floor that the ranch rested on.

"Come back fast!" Lucy yelled "Its okay that I have him come in fast, right, Ray?" Lucy yelled as she picked up her camera, readying for the shot.

"Only if it turns out great, Red!" Ray hollered back.

Terry came through the thick brush atop a rusty colored roan like a cannon ball straight out of a cannon. Just then a quick wind blew through the camp, making the mane of the beautiful horse fly in all directions as Terry came up on Lucy and then blew by her. She could feel the intensity of his eyes as the Cowboy looked straight into her lens, and Lucy knew by the racing in her heart, that she had indeed, captured something extraordinary.

It was at that precise moment that the once well known photographer realized that Marcie was nowhere to be seen.

"Julie!" Lucille yelled to the long legged young blonde dismounting her horse in true fashion. "Where's Marcie?"

"Who's Marcie?" Julie responded innocently as she shielded her eyes from the morning sun and looked out towards Lucille.

"Are you kidding me?" Lucy said - trying hard to suppress a giggle in case Julie actually really didn't remember who Marcie was.

115

"Yassss! HAHAHAHAHA!" Julie laughed aloud. "I'm sorry! Riding this horse just turns my mind to mush and before I know it I'm working up comedy in my crazy mind, and I think I'm funny!" Julie continued through a big beautiful smile, laughing as she untied her stampede string that held her hat on her head.

"Well you ARE funny!" Deb said as she walked up beside Julie and motioned for Lucille to come join them under the Mesquite tree.

"You got my goat, Julie, that's for sure" Lucy said through genuine laughter as she quickly hugged the two good morning.

"Welp, sorry about your friend, but I'm starving and you know how it is, save yourself, right?" Julie said as she made a beeline for the breakfast line that the remaining ladies had already formed.

"Yep, every man for herself!" Deb said laughing at her own joke, as she quickly followed Julie to the line of hungry and chatty cowgirls.

"Now wait just one minute!" Lucille yelled "Somebody needs to tell me where Marcie is for God's sake!"

"Terry sent her out looking for her horse Diamond Ring — Green chimed in, she got loose this morning somehow, and Marcie insisted she be located; so that old man put her up on Matilda's horse, slapped that mare on the ass and sent her out searching." Green said to the now shocked redhead as he walked up beside her, cupped her elbow in his hand and guided her towards the other ladies.

"Well she can't be out there by herself, can she, Green?" Lucille asked in a very serious tone.

"She's not out there by herself, Red" Ray chimed in. "She's on Matilda's horse. And when you're lucky enough to ride THAT horse, you're lucky enough." He continued. "She'll find Diamond Ring, and the three of 'em will be back before the last of you get served, so don't you worry that pretty little head of yours, Miss Lucy; Marcie is in good hands."

"With ALLSTATE!" Trish yelled, cackling as she sat herself down in one of the lawn chairs that Sam and Eileen had placed in a circle. Everybody laughed as hard as anyone could laugh, and soon each lady was seated in a chair, plates on their laps, and black coffee in metal cups on stumps next to them.

"Dig in, ladies!" Terry said as he sat down amongst them all.

And dig in they did.

Green and Lucille opted for seats opposite most of the ladies, but next to Terry; and soon everyone was raving about the freshly cooked breakfast through mouthfuls of cheese eggs, biscuits and gravy, and bacon.

Sitting there next to Green and Terry, watching her newfound lady friends talk amongst each other as though they'd all grown up together, Lucille caught herself thinking how much she'd love to just stay here forever, and how much she was falling in love with Green.

As her mind wandered off towards thoughts of the two of them wrangling together on this very ranch, Green reached out with her other camera he'd been holding, tapped her on the knee with it and said "might want to grab a few shots of breakfast, young lady."

Lucille, jarred from her crazy thoughts of a future that would most likely never be, quickly grabbed the camera from Green, handed him her still full plate, and waltzed over to the cooking fires, and began photographing what was left of breakfast in the cast iron pots and pans.

Turning around she saw Green watching her, so she lifted her camera to her eye and snapped off a few shots of the blonde mustached cowboy in his red silk scarf, black cowboy hat with tan ribbing, and a hawk's feather placed perfectly in the thin leather hat band. Lucy caught her breath with each snap of the shutter, as Green stared right into her soul, his eyes an icy blue, now filling with desire as she continued to press and release the shutter button. Her heart began racing so quickly that she told herself to put her camera down, and she did. But Green was still staring intently at her, and she was feeling a fire burning in areas she had long forgotten about.

"Damnit if there was no one else but the two of us, and I wasn't married to an asshole, I don't think I could keep myself away from that man right now" Lucy said to herself, completely forgetting her surroundings as her eyes held Green's, and then succumbing to the guilt that soon followed after having such thoughts as a married woman.

"Come and finish your breakfast, Red" Green said, shaking her from the trance she was in. Embarrassed at the thought that the others might have noticed her emotions, she quickly resumed her position in her chair and began eating what was still on her plate.

117

"You get some good shots of my fat ass dismounting, Lucy?" Trish yelled, as the others chimed in asking if she had gotten any good shots of their back ends, too.

"Hahaha!" Lucille laughed, almost spitting her coffee out as she did so. "You guys slay me!" She continued, thankful for the much needed humor.

"Yassss I got all you alls asses right here in the memory of my trusty Nikon, ladies!" Lucy said through laughter.

As all the ladies whooped and hollered at the comedy of it all, Sam hollered out "Lucy its "Y'alls," not "You Alls! If you're gonna try to speak like a Texan, speak like a Texan!" Sam continued through light laughter, winking at the still giggling redhead sitting beside Green, who, unbeknownst to Lucille, was Sam's Godfather. But that's another story for another time.

"Well I've never been to Texas in my life, Sam!" Lucille laughed. "I guess if I'm going to come visit you one day, I better get my lingo down!"

"I would LOVE it if you and Green would come visit me when/if I go back there" Sam said as she walked over to the horses with Eileen, and began watering them at a trough that had been purposely placed there for the breakfast rides that happened on every Dusty Bar Trails weeklong trip.

Terry and Green instructed the ladies to pack up their paper plates and plastic utensils, and place them in the black bag that was being passed around, encouraged everyone to grab a bottle of water out of the ice chest that was sitting next to the Chuck Wagon that had carried all of the food and cooking utensils etc., and gave a heads up that all would be saddling up in half an hour.

It was just then that Marcie showed up atop Matilda's horse, looking radiantly beautiful under a black cowboy hat, and a Royal Blue silk scarf she'd tied beautifully around her neck.

"I found Diamond Ring!" She exclaimed (just a little too excitedly, Lucy thought to herself) to all the ladies as they gathered round her. And sure enough there was Marcie's ride for the week, ponied up alongside Matilda's horse.

Marcie dismounted as Terry walked up and took both horses from her, and walked them over to the watering trough. "Grab some breakfast, little lady" Terry said as he winked at her, touched her shoulder and guided her in the direction of what was left of the food.

"Well! Don't mind if I do!" Marcie stated emphatically as she filled up her plate and began to eat.

"You can say that again" Terry said to Marcie as he walked away.

"Which part?" Marcie yelled after him.

"The 'I do' part" Terry said over his shoulder as he continued to walk towards the group's horses.

"Cup ah coffee o' Best friend o' mine?" Lucy said, handing the overly zealous and smiling Marcie a steaming cup of black coffee.

"Mmmm, mmm hmmm, yes" Marcie said through a mouthful of eggs.

"Did you hear what Terry just said to you?" Lucy asked Marcie.

"Mmm hmmm yes I did" Marcie said as she continued to eat.

"Well don't you find that a little intriguing?"

"What?"

"What Terry just said!" Lucy exclaimed.

"You know, no... I really don't actually. I mean after finding a Diamond Ring attached to the saddle of Diamond Ring that I found when I finally found Diamond Ring, no... I don't find his comment intriguing at all." Marcie said, still shoveling forkfuls of cheese eggs, biscuits and bacon into her mouth.

"What's intriguing to me is whether or not I should say yes."

Lucille's jaw dropped to the desert floor, and she wasn't sure she'd ever be able to pick it back up from what felt like a suddenly permanently open position.

Before Lucy could even respond, Green brought Lucky up to her and told her it was time to saddle up.

"Now wait a minute Green, I've got to finish talking to Marcie" Lucille pleaded.

119

"No, no… you go on ahead Lucy, I've got this." The brunette said as nonchalantly as if she'd just told her to pick up some milk for her at the grocer.

Green, out of sight of Matilda and Ray, slapped Lucille as hard as he could on her ass and said "Now git up on that horse before you make us all late for nap-time, lady!"

Lucy, realizing the atmosphere was lighter than she was previously perceiving it after Marcie's side comment, laughed and saddled up, winked at her best friend and said "Ah to heck with it, Marcie! You're almost 50 years old! Say YES!"

With a click of her tongue and squeeze of her heels, she moved Lucky out into a fast trot back into the brush that the ladies had come out from.

Green swung himself up onto his horse, and slowly walked towards the direction of Lucille, watching as each gal followed behind her on their respective horses, yelling like the bunch of cowgirls they believed themselves to be.

Green thought to himself that if ever there was a finer group of cowgirls to be had, it was each one of them; and in particular, Lucille.

Clicking his mare into a fast trot, Green quickly took the lead from Lucy and slowed the whole gang to a walk, congratulating each lady on their horsemanship and riding skills over the last few days as they meandered back down onto the floor of the dry riverbed, and made their way back to the corrals.

Chapter 14

"Who wants to head back to the ranch kitchen and celebrate with a few home brewed beers, brought to you by Ray himself?" Green asked the ladies.

"Well we ALL do!" Trish yelled. "Right ladies?"

"RIGHT!" They all said in unison. Save for Lucy who knew the innocence of the suggestion and so rolled along with the moment, without speaking up.

"That's great!" A rough voice other than Green's called out.

Riding up amongst them, with Marcie at his side Terry yelled "You can all help me clean up the kitchen when the chuck wagon arrives, and you can partake in those beers AFTER the afternoon ride."

"Yaaaaaay for Beer!" Julie yelled as she trotted past the bewildered cowboy.

"Julie!" Trish yelled after the smiling, and completely clueless blonde. "He said AFTER the Afternoon Ride, which is AFTER we SLAVE in the kitchen on a dude ranch that we PAID to be on!"

But Julie just kept trotting away — heading towards the opening of the corrals, whimsically singing "99 Tootles of Beer on the wall."

"Its BOTTLES!" Every single woman in the group said out loud at the same time.

Terry just shook his head and laughed as he waved the ladies past him, Marcie included; making sure each one of them were under the sign before he himself walked his horse under it. Reaching up to touch the metal with his fingertips, Terry sent up a little prayer to heaven. "Father, let her say yes, but most of all let her make the decision that's best for her. But let her say yes." After a quick moment of silence, Terry nudged the roan under the sign, and on into the corrals.

After dismounting his horse, and handing off the reigns to the kitchen gals who sometimes assisted in the corrals, Terry made sure to give orders to Sam as to which horse needed what, and to remember to lock the gate after she let them out to pasture.

"That darned Diamond Ring" He said to Sam. "She sure likes playing Houdini."

"Well let's hope that wild brunette doesn't, eh Terry?" Sam said, winking at him as she walked on by.

"You're a little too old for those britches, missy." Terry called after the Texas Cowgirl.

"Nah" Sam said. "I just have an intuition that plays out like a fiddle playing Orange Blossom Special, Terry."

Terry just shook his head, smiled and headed towards the kitchen area through the front door of the dining hall.

"Terry!" Trish whispered before he could make it across the room to the kitchen.

"TERRY!" She whispered louder, tripping over the leg of a chair as she quickly made her way to him.

Terry turned slowly around.

"You here to help clean up, Little Lady?"

"You gonna pay me?" The older woman cackled.

"Nope. What's on your mind?" He smiled, knowing the question that was about to be popped from the loud and boisterous woman that he couldn't help but adore.

"We don't want to ride this afternoon." Marcie chimed in, pretending to stand at attention as she and the rest of the ladies poured into the dining area, and sidled up alongside the ever smiling Trish.

"Yeah" said Trish, "we want to lay around the pool and sip lemonade," she continued in what Terry thought was a very convincing English accent.

Trish batted her eyes at the Cowboy and made a motion with her right hand as though quaintly lifting a tiny teacup to her lips, pinky sticking straight out.

"Well ladies, do what you want, if you're that lazy" Terry said.

Before he could finish saying another word, all the women voiced quickly in agreement at just how lazy they were, as they hurried themselves out the door to their respective bunkhouses, discussing what bathing suits each woman was going to wear, and who was going to spike the lemonade.

Miss Marcie, a minute please, ma'am?" Terry said just before Marcie could skirt out the door.

"Yes, Rhett?" Marcie said as she stood in the doorway, unsure if she should tease the tall cowboy, or crumble at the sight of him.

"Did you find what you were looking for out there in the desert this morning?" He inquired towards the raving beauty.

"Do you realize what you're asking me, Terry?"

"I do" he said as he turned and walked through the swinging doors into the kitchen.

Marcie just kept smiling as she turned and walked out the door, and headed towards her bunkhouse so she could get ready for an afternoon of what would surely be filled with laughter. Marcie knew how she wanted to respond. She also knew that she wasn't going to do so in an off the cuff moment.

Terry met Green in the kitchen. "How'd we get roped into kitchen duty?" he said to the blonde cowboy leaning up against the front of a big industrial sized, stainless steel refrigerator.

"The Kitchen Girls took the rest of the afternoon off, so after handling the horses, they all went to some photography art-show in town," Green said, while chewing on a toothpick.

"Humpf" mumbled Terry as he quickly took to cleaning up the remnants from the morning meal.

Terry could feel Green's eyes on him as he ran hot steamy water over what was left of the stainless steel cooking utensils in the sink.

"What are you thinking, Old Boy?" Terry said without looking up from his chore.

"Well, Old Man" Green drawled. "I was thinking that I think you've got yourself thinking, that one gal in particular has actually got you thinking."

Terry laughed as he reached up and turned the water off, and then turned towards Green.

"And what are you thinking about that gal of yours, who I'm sure is thinking she isn't quite sure what to think of a man of your thinking capabilities" Terry said solidly but with a wide smile, as he eyed Green.

Green smiled wide and just kept chewing on his toothpick, looking right back at Terry.

"Cat got your tongue?", Terry inquired.

"Yup" was all Green said as he pushed himself away from the refrigerator, walked right past Terry, and out the kitchen door.

"We're both in a heap of trouble, you know that, Old Boy, right?" Terry yelled after Green.

"Trouble isn't what I'd call it, Old Man." Green yelled back as he walked out the front door.

"Well whaddya call it, then?" Terry yelled. But Green was already out of earshot, and Terry knew it.

"Ah hell" Terry said to no one in particular, as he began to dry and put the clean dishes away. "Damn gals got both our hearts wrapped up."

Chapter 15

"HEYY! QUIT IT YOU CRAZIES!" Lucille's agitated screams could be heard from across the ranch as Marcie, Trish, and Julie finally grabbed hold of the wildly swinging woman and positioned themselves to toss the fiery red head into the waiting waters of the Dusty Bar Trails swimming pool.

Trish and Julie held the squirming arms of Lucille, as Marcie tried feverishly to maintain a good hold on her ankles. Just as Marcie was about to lose her grip, a large hand reached out of nowhere and grabbed hold of Lucille's kicking left foot.

"GREEN!" Lucille screamed, wide eyed at the cowboy who had suddenly joined in on the commotion of throwing her into the waters below. "I CANNOT SWIM! MARCIE TELL THEM I CANNOT SWIM!"

"You're about to learn, cowgirl!" Green yelled as Marcie laughingly counted to three and gave a heave ho, as the four of them tossed the dust-covered woman in the pool.

Into the pool water Lucille went with a splash. Emerging from the water, she coughed, sputtered, and laughed all at the same time, wiping mercilessly at the chlorinated water stinging her now wide open eyes.

"You sons of....why I'm going to get each and every one of you back!" She yelled boisterously above the laughter of the others hanging round the pools edge, laughing at the comedic movements of Lucille as she made her way to the side of the pool, and hoisted herself up into a sitting position on the edge.

"Somebody come get these cowboy boots off of me before they are stuck on my feet forever!" She pleaded.

Green came to the rescue, taking his hat off and nodding his head to the wet redhead, he grabbed hold of her right boot and began to pull. Before anyone could so much as bat an eyelash, the boot came off in Green's hands and with one good push Lucile sent the surprised cowboy, sprawling ass over tea kettle, right into the pool.

Lucille jumped up from her sitting position at the precise moment that the head wrangler emerged from the cold waters, sprang across the pool yard, up and over the gated fence, and sprinted off to the safety of her cabin, one boot on, and one boot off.

As Lucille sat on the edge of her bed, failing miserably at removing her left boot, Marcie raced in through the cabin door, slamming it shut behind her and locking it.

"Are you absolutely insane?" Marcie said through a wide grin.

"Was he mad?" Lucille asked the wide eyed girl, in as innocent a tone as possible.

"Madder than a wet hen, you crazy old cowgirl!" Marcie said as she pulled the boot off of Lucille's soaked foot.

The two laid back on the bed together and laughed for a few minutes before Lucille decided it was time to get showered and cleaned up for supper. The girls realized they'd had so much fun at the pool, they were bound to miss appetizer hour, and they were starving.

Back in the dining hall, Ray was setting out dinner plates in preparation for a feast of grilled tri-tip, lobster tail, and potatoes, that as with all meals on the ranch, he had prepared himself.

Terry and Green, quiet as two church mice, walked in to help Ray finish setting up. Ray looked knowingly at the two cowboys, noticing the glint in each set of eyes as they quickly got to work.

"You know this visit is coming to a close, boys..." Ray said as he made his way back to the kitchen.

Three days seemed to fly by. Neither cowboy said a word as Ray disappeared through the swinging doors, only to reappear with a bottle of Jack Daniels and three glasses filled with ice.

"Cop a squat boys, and let's have a chat, I smell change coming in the air from both of you" the older cowboy stated as he slid out two chairs at the head table, motioned for each of the men to sit, placed a glass in front of each of them and made himself a seat at the head of the table, Terry on his right, and Green on his left.

All three men were quiet as their Ranch Boss poured a hefty shot of whiskey over the ice filled glasses, then picked his up and motioned for the two men seated on either side of him, to do the same.

"To change" was all Ray needed to say, and all three men clinked their glasses together and took a big swallow of the now ice cold whiskey.

Terry swirled the ice around in his glass and sat it down on the table; breaking the silence he said "I don't think I can let this one go without a good old fashioned try, boss."

Ray just looked at Terry as a knowing smile crept across his face.

"That's not new news to me, Terry," He said, winking at Green as the younger cowboy also took his turn at setting his now empty glass down on the table.

Green broke the silence this time. Leaning back in his chair he placed a toothpick in the corner of his mouth and said, "I'm taking Miss Lucy back to Wyoming with me boss, and if it's all the same to you, I'd like to do so at the end of my term here, if she'll agree to stay that long."

Terry and Ray looked at each other, and Green could sense that they both knew something that he didn't know.

"Well, boys" Ray said as he pushed himself back from the table and stood up. "Best get that Dining Room in order, those crazy ladies will be showing up for supper before we know it."

With that being said, Terry and Green also stood up and walked back into the dining room with Ray in the lead.

Chapter 16

Lucille stepped out of the shower and began toweling off her hair as Marcie moved on by her to take her turn under the spray.

Blow drying her hair in the mirror, Lucille recalled the butterflies she felt when she looked up into Green's eyes as he bent over to pull her boot off in the pool area. She wondered if he'd felt the same spark. She felt like he was staring right into her soul, and decided as she turned the dryer off, that the stare he gave her, was precisely the reason that she found the courage to give him one swift push into the pool.

Laughing at the memory, Lucille quickly braided her hair into a tail that laid beautiful and full over her left shoulder, applied a light lipstick and a quick coat of 3D mascara, pulled on a pair of blue jeans, white t-shirt and her boots; and skirted out the door before Marcie was finished showering.

Heading towards the great room in the main house where appetizers were sure to be well underway with the rest of the gang, Lucille heard the soft nicker of a horse.

Lucky was standing alone in the gated area of the corrals, saddled up and ready to go. A note attached to the horn of his saddle read "thought you might enjoy a lone early evening ride before supper. Don't be long, see you when you get back. Love, Your New Future (if you are so inclined.)" Lucille smiled at Green's signature.

Well Lucky, Lucille softly said to the waiting horse. We'll miss appetizers, but might as well take advantage. With a quick leg up over the saddle, she positioned herself in the stirrups, nudged Lucky closer to the panel he was tied to, released the rope and reigned the horse she had fallen in love with, out towards the opening of the corral.

Just as soon as she crossed under the sign, Lucille reached up and touched the bottom of it, gave Lucky a quick squeeze with her heels and began a soft trot out over the desert floor of Wickenburg. She always loved the way he could trot, just enough speed to go nowhere fast, with very little bounce.

When they reached the sandy bottom of the Hassayampa river, she gave another quick squeeze, clicking her tongue a few times as Lucky broke out into a slow lope, carrying her through the twists and turns of the pathway carved out by the spring waters that during the wet months, could flow insanely fast. But not this time of year, this time of year you could ride for miles on the sandy bottom, and it was fabulous.

She let Lucky carry her, as she relished in the way the hot Arizona evening sun felt on her face, as a light wind began to blow, loosening the braid in her hair.

Everywhere around her a golden hue was pouring out across the desert as the sun made its last but greatest attempt in shining brilliantly as it slowly dipped behind the mountains. Lucille knew she should head back soon, supper was always just after sunset, but first she had to experience this brilliance before her. She slowed Lucky to a stop, then sat there atop the amazing animal that she connected with so seamlessly, and watched the sun's rays make their longest crawl across the desert floor.

As the colors of the evening went from pinks and blues and orange, to muted purples and sage greens, Lucille nudged Lucky forward into a leisurely walk as she made her way back to the corrals; keenly aware of the grumbling in her stomach as she thought about the suppertime ahead.

Marcie met Lucille as she exited the corrals, and without a word hooked arms together and headed in the direction of the Dining Hall where the smell of steamed seafood and grilled steak was pungent on the air.

"Appetizers were good, my friend?" Lucy asked Marcie.

"Everybody except Trish, Deb and Julie, slept through them" Marcie laughed. "Including me!"

"Ladieeee-eeeee-hooo-hooooooo!!! Oh Lovely Laiiiiddddiiieeessss" came a squeaky but loud sing song of a voice across the air. Lucille and Marcie turned around to see Trish waving and waddling in their direction, the rest of the gals in tow.

"Well hey there, sexy cowgirl!" Marcie yelled over to Trish.

"More like fat, stuffed, and out of breath cowgirl!" Trish said as she and the other gals sidled up alongside and around the duo.

"You ladies sure missed one helluv an appetizer night" Deb chimed in. They had all kinds of whores Dee ovaries AND Gin and Tonics WITH the juiciest limes!" Deb said, laughing at her own twist on words, as she came up beside the two.

"Oh yes, it was wonderHIC - wonderful" Julie said as she covered her mouth with her hand and giggled.

"I'm sure we did, dangit!" Marcie said as she smiled at everyone. "And now I'm starving!"

"And THIRSTY!" Lucille chimed in. "You ladies smell like a distillery!"

"Like as in hic-water?" Julie said, failing miserably at keeping a straight face.

"Because if that was distilled water, then I must be allergic to it, becau-hic because it got me hic D - R - U - N - C - hic -

Julie spelled out the word drunk, in between hiccups, except she used the letter C instead of a K, and try as everyone may, nobody could keep themselves from howling and bowling over in laughter as they all made their way into the dining hall.

"Well look what the circus brought to town" Ray said as he welcomed each of the ladies, and ushered them towards the big pine wood rustic dining table. "We've got quite the feast for you ladies tonight, I sure hope you brought your appetites"

"I brought my appetite AND a drunk blonde!" Trish exclaimed as she pulled out a chair for Julie and guided her down into it.

Pulling out her own chair next to the giggling blonde, Trish sat down with a thump and said "I could eat a horse!" Followed quickly by uproarious laughter from everyone as they sat in their respective seats.

Green was the first to bring out the beginnings of the main course for the evening; walking around the table to each lady (each of whom was dressed to the hilt in the most trending jeans, tops and western jewelry accessories) and placed a giant whole Maine Lobster on each plate. Ooohs and ahhhhhs were a plenty as drawn butter was then placed at each of the gals' plates, by Sam, looking positively radiant in her 21 years of age.

"Boy when I was your age, I would have died to work at a place like this" Marcie said to the young girl who was dressed in tight fitting jeans, red cowboy boots and a matching top to boot. She wore turquoise jewelry complete with a chunky silver cross necklace.

"I love it here so much, I'm pretty lucky that my Uncle owns the place!" She beamed as she looked over at Ray and Matilda, who were just seating themselves in their respective places at the table.

"Yes ma'am ladies, that there is my Niece 'Samantha,' and she's the prettiest thing this side of the Mississippi." Ray continued on as he looked fondly upon the young lady setting the last dish of butter down by Marcie.

"You remind me of me, when I was your age, Samantha" Marcie said to the young lady.

"Well I'll take that as a compliment, and hope I look as beautiful as you do now, please feel free to call me Sam." Sam said as she winked at Marcie.

"Does any of y'all need anything else before I head back to the kitchen?" Sam said as she looked around at each woman, taking in the unique qualities of each of them before her.

"A tall drink of water, if he's back there!" Marcie said with a wide smile.

Sam just laughed and said she'd be returning with bottles of Chardonnay and Iced Tea, and that Terry and Green would be bringing out platters of tri-tip along with potatoes au-gratin, to be passed around.

As the ladies began to crack open their lobsters, Terry and Green waltzed into the dining room, each carrying the platters of food, and each with a towel draped over their arms "Concierge style" Terry said as he smiled and winked at Marcie.

After all the plates were served, and the cracked shells from the lobster were cleared from the table by Sam, all the ladies began to dig in. Not a word was said as each woman began to sample the lobster, and then the tri-tip, only the scraping of forks on plates could be heard as suppertime was officially in full swing.

Marcie was drinking Chardonnay along with the other ladies, encouraged to do so by Lucille who whispered to the brunette to "stop worrying so much" while she enjoyed a tall glass of Iced Tea complete with a lime that Sam had popped in her drink one of the times she passed by the table.

"That's some Niece you've got there, Ray and Matilda" Lucille said to the handsome couple. "Has she always had that adorable southern drawl?" She asked.

"Texas, my dear! Born and raised there by my Brother and his wife. Big time cattle ranchers in the Lonestar state, but she likes Arizona better." Ray said as he winked at Matilda, and squeezed her knee.

Matilda, who was often quiet, but always sweet, smiled a big grin and said, "and we're sure glad to have her here with us."

"Is she just summer help, like last year?" Lucille continued as she took a bite of the tender lobster she had just submerged in butter.

"It started out that way, but she'll be with us for awhile now while the family goes through some adjustments." Matilda said.

Lucille could see a shadow cross her eyes as she looked at Ray, who try as he may, couldn't hide a fleeting look of sadness that crossed his face as he smiled and said "Well eat up there young lady, Green told me you'd be might starved by the time you got back from your lone-rider ride, my dear."

And with that he took a big bite of ti-tip, slugged down a good gulp of the yellow buttery flavored wine, and made a bee-line with his fork for a big piece of lobster he had left lying in his melted butter dish. Lucille decided that it was clear something tragic had either happened, or was happening, and made a mental note not to bring it up again."

"Mmmmm MMMMMM!" Ray said as he looked around the table. "Now ain't this some of the best seafood you'd of ever thunk you'd have in the desert, ladies?"

Trish was the first to respond as she swallowed a piece herself. "Well hot dog, Ray! I guess I never even considered just where you might get such fresh lobster from in this part of the country!" She said with a twinkle in her eye.

"Sure hope I don't get food poisoning!" She cackled as she slurped down another piece of the white tender flesh. "I don't care if I do, you know! This oversized flea is Deeeeeeeeeee-VINE!" Trish emphasized on the word as she plunked another piece of lobster in her mouth.

Deb and Julie and the rest of the gals all chimed in that it indeed was the very best Lobster they had ever eaten, "And not just in the desert!" Lucille said as she herself finished off another bite.

As the evening drew on, and each lady finished their plate, Lucille surprised herself by suddenly realizing that Green and Terry never came back to the table to eat. Kicking Marcie in the shin to get her attention she whispered, "Where do you think Terry and Green are, Marcie?"

But Marcie just shrugged her shoulders and said "well how would I know? I'm not their keeper."

Lucille just stared at Marcie, and Marcie knew that her best friend would get up and leave if she didn't correct herself right then and there.

"Honey" Marcie said. "Terry said that he and Green were going to do some cussing and discussing about some things they needed to cuss and discuss, along with a few other topics that needed to be talked out, mainly me and you, and that's all I know" she said as she leaned over and gave a quick peck on Lucille's cheek.

"So don't you worry your pretty head, I promise you that Green isn't giving you the cold shoulder."

"I didn't insinuate that, Marcie"

"Yes, you did"

"No, I didn't" Lucille whispered through gritted teeth.

While Marcie was wondering what might have gotten Lucille's panties in a bunch, it suddenly dawned on her that she hadn't finished telling Lucy what she promised she'd finish telling her, before leaving her with Green at the Bon Fire.

It also just dawned on her that her best friend of 20 years hadn't even brought it up again, which meant that she was seething inside, which also meant that she should probably let the cat out of the bag, before Lucille let her imagination go into over-drive.

"Too late" Lucille said. As though reading Marcie's mind.

Before Marcie could utter a word, Lucy stood up from the table, told the ladies she would meet them at the nightly bon fire in a little bit after freshening up, nodded to Ray and Matilda, and headed out the dining room door.

Marcie couldn't get up fast enough, but not before spooning in the last mouthful of au-gratins and gulping down the rest of her wine.
"Freshen up, my ass" Marcie said to the surprised group as she slammed her now empty glass down on the table.

"If I'm not back in 20 come find me." She said as she marched out after Lucille.

"Well, and here I thought those two were straight as a bone!" Trish cackled out loud as she raised her glass in front of her nose, sniffed in the sweet smell of the luscious golden liquid, swirled the glass in front of her like a magician, and before taking a healthy gulp, said "Just kidding, I know a lovers' quarrel when I see one, and that ain't one!"

Putting her now empty glass down on the table, Trish said to the ladies and Ray and Matilda "Looks like it's time for Mother Hubbard to kick in and go knock some heads together" the older and still jovial woman said.

Clicking her heels together like the scarecrow on the Wizard of Oz, Trish skipped off across the dining room floor, and out the door.

Before closing it behind her she stuck her head back through, grabbed a full bottle of Chardonnay off the buffet that was beside the door, winked and said, "If I'm not back in 20!"

Everyone could hear her cackling even as she closed the door behind her.

Deb, quietly eyeing everyone at the table with a sly smile said aloud "any takers that this is about a man?"

"Oh it's not about a man, y'all" a voice said from the kitchen.   "It's about a real bonafide cowboy who probably knows more than that pretty little red headed filly friend of yours does!"

All the ladies turned around to see that the voice came from Sam, who was now waltzing back into the dining room, Terry in tow, carrying a tray each of "after dinner" port wine, and slices of cheesecake for all.

"Well she sure doesn't know everything, cuz I'm about to eat her cheesecake!" Julie said - still feeling a little funny after her Gin and Tonics and two glasses of Chardonnay. She grabbed a glass of Port Wine off of Terry's tray and said to the smiling cowboy "Is this homemade?"

"No ma'am it's an after dinner drink called "Port Wine." The tall cowboy said.
"Oh!" Julie said as she winked at the other ladies. "Totally thought it was cheesecake" and downed the glass in one fell swoop.

All the ladies joined in the fun of partaking in the desert wine along with a luscious slice of blueberry cheesecake each, as Ray and Matilda bid their goodnights to all, and strolled out the dining room door, hand in hand.

Well ladies, we've got time for a few songs under the stars and an hour or so of bon fire time before you all should consider retiring for the night. Sam and the kitchen staff will clear your places; morning comes early and so does the last morning ride. I'll see you at the fire pit." Terry tipped his hat and skidded out the door quickly.

"Well that was quick!" Julie said as her eyes followed Terry out the door.

"A little too quick if you ask me, for someone who was just going to strum a few strings for a bunch of old ladies tonight." Deb chimed in.

"I know, right?" Julie said as she hooked her arm through Deb's and motioned for the other ladies to follow as they all headed out the door behind Terry, making their way to the familiar log stumps, and orange glow of the bon-fire in the distance.

Chapter 17

Trish stopped about twenty feet from the parking lot where Marcie was standing with her hands on her hips, neck stuck out like a rooster, and crowing just as loud as one.

"Well I think Mother Hubbard best just stay put" said Terry to Trish, as he came up quickly behind her.

"You bring the popcorn for this show, Cowboy?" Trish whispered to Terry, neither of them taking their eyes off the scene playing out before them as they hid in the shadows of the main house porch.

"Nope, but I brought dessert" said the Cowboy as he handed a half full bottle of Port to Trish, held two glasses while she poured and copped a squat on the porch, motioning for the jovial gal to join him as Marcie began a tirade that was too good to miss.

"LUCILLE MADISON YOU STOP RIGHT NOW! I CAN NOT RUN IN THESE BOOTS!" Marcie yelled as she quick stepped after her friend who was making a fast beeline for Marcie's truck in the parking lot.

"I AM TELLING YOU IF YOU DON'T STOP I AM GOING TO WHIP A ROCK RIGHT AT YOUR HEAD!" She yelled as her friend continued on, clearly intent on making it to the truck before Marcie could stop her.

"Are you SERIOUS?" Marcie yelled as she made a quick left and bounded off towards their bunkhouse, barreled through the door, grabbed the spare set of keys she always kept in her purse (she hadn't removed the key from her truck's ignition since she bought it ten years ago,) walked triumphantly back onto the front step and clicked the Lock Button key on her remote with a wave of her arm that even Glenda the good witch herself couldn't compete with.

"Take THAT!" She yelled to absolutely NO-ONE.

Lucille had literally disappeared into thin air.

"LUCY MAY!" Marcie yelled into the thin air. She always changed her best friend's middle name when she was mad at her.

And ever so slowly as her eyes adjusted in the low light of the white security light that stood tall over the dirt lot, she could see Lucy peering at her from behind the steering wheel. She was hunkered down so that only her eyes and the top part of her head could be seen beneath the top part of the steering wheel through the windshield as Marcie stomped up to the truck and clicked the Unlock Button on the remote. Reaching out to grab the door handle she heard a click as Lucille locked the doors from the inside.

Marcie immediately went to the front of the old truck, popped the hood and with one fell swoop, disconnected the battery just as Lucy was about to turn the key.

"If you will just give me a minute of your precious time, I will explain everything" Marcie yelled as she walked back up to the driver's side window. "Now unlock the doors!"

"No!" Lucille said as she sat straight up in the driver's seat.

"DO IT, DO IT NOW!" Marcie commanded, using the terminology she taught to Police Explorers at the annual Police Explorers Academy years ago when she lived in Michigan.

Cranking down the window just enough to be able to get her lips up to, Lucy yelled "Do you see a big yellow E, ANYWHERE on my shirt, Marcie?"

"OPEN THE DAMN DOOR OR I PROMISE YOU I WILL BREAK THIS WINDOW" and with that, Marcie, knowing full well that Lucy would certainly NOT unlock the doors, bent over, picked up a rock and drew back.

"ALRIGHT! ALRIGHT!" Lucy yelled as she crank rolled down the window the rest of the way. "Hook the damn battery back up so I can unlock the doors"

"Oh for the love of PETE!" Marcie said as she reached in through the window in a valiant attempt to hit the unlock button.

Click. Nothing.

"I'd lift the knob up manually, but I broke it off" Lucille said as she leaned her chin on her forearms folded over the open window, and batted her eyelashes at Marcie.

"Shit" was all the brunette could say.

"Go hook the battery back up, Marcie." Lucille said sarcastically.

"Don't you dare move a muscle" Marcie said as she made her way back to the front of the truck and hooked up the battery.

Click — Lucille unlocked the doors and clamored out of the truck, emotionally spent from her yelling match with Marcie, but oddly giddy at the notion that she and her best friend could banter like this, and still remain somewhat calm, and still remain friends.

Lucy leaned up against the old truck and took a pack of cigarettes out of her back pocket, and lit up two, passing one to Marcie, who took a long drag and then joined Lucy, leaning up against the truck and watching the ladies in the distance while a soft guitar could be heard strumming "Country Roads".

"Come on Luce, lets go join the gang before it gets too late" Marcie said as she took another drag from her cigarette and pushed herself away from the truck.

"No Marcie, I'm not moving a muscle until you tell me what is going on, and don't dilly daly, just spill it" Lucy said - her eyes darkening as she pleaded with the one person who never held a thing back from her.

"Hank filed for a 30 day divorce, Lucy. Its published in the local paper".

Before Lucy could ask the question, Marcie continued "the fucker mailed it to this ranch, attention 'Me'."

The silence that followed was loud enough to wake the dead.

"Lucy?"

"Just give me a minute" Lucille whispered as she closed her eyes and leaned her head back against the metal that separated the cab from the bed of the truck.

"What in the actual fuck did you just say to me, Marce?" Was all that she could muster.

"I said that Hank filed for a 30 days divorce, and published it in the local paper."

"That's what I thought you said" Lucy whispered. Her eyes still closed as she took another long drag off of her cigarette.

"Well don't you want to know when?" Marcie quietly said.

"Not really, though its been at least a week because I'm pretty sure you knew before you even picked me up at my godforsaken house."

"No, I didn't know, Lucy" Marcie quietly said.

"You love that house, honey" she continued.

"Not anymore I don't." Lucy whispered.

"Lucy" Marcie began… but Lucille just held up her hand, and as if on que, Marcie clammed up.

As Lucille wracked her brain over and over again asking silently to herself the question "how in thee HELL did I not know about this?" followed by "and what the hell is HE divorcing ME for?" followed by a slow and maddening desire to scream; a new song could be heard on the guitar in the distance, and Lucy bent over at the waist and began to sob as she heard the ladies around the bonfire in faint voices break into the famous chorus line from John Denver's "Sunshine on my Shoulders."

For the first time in their relationship, Marcie did, and said, absolutely nothing at all as Lucy straightened up, handed her what was left of her cigarette, headed towards the bunkhouse, up onto the porch, and through the bedroom door; shutting it quietly behind her.

Just then a voice from behind Marcie quietly said "Come on Miss Marcie, lets go join the ladies." Green stepped out of the darkness towards her, and Marcie allowed him to take her elbow, and steer her in the direction of the music and the group of ladies she suddenly and desperately needed to be around.

Terry and Trish, deciding their exit when Lucy got down out of the truck, not wanting to make any sort of mistake in giving themselves away, had already made their way back to the bon fire, where Terry quickly began playing the soft tune.

As Green and Marcie made their way towards the glow of the fire, Terry stopped strumming and handed his guitar off to Julie, who much to everyone's surprise, started slowly playing an old Kenny Loggins tune called "Christopher Robbins".

"Dance in the firelight, Scarlett?" Terry said to Marcie, knowing she'd need his arms around her.

Before Marcie could respond, Terry had her in his arms in true cowboy fashion, and swung her slowly in a circle as Julie began to sing the lyrics to the song that even she herself remembered as a child.

"I take it she knows now, eh pretty lady?" Terry whispered to Marcie, his lips gently pressed against her forehead as he spoke.

"That she does, Terry. That she does" was all Marcie could muster as she rested her head on his shoulder, and let him gently sway her to the music as the ladies joined in the song singing "help me if you can, I've got to get back to the house at Pooh corner by one."

And that's when Trish decided it was high time to switch up the atmosphere as she instructed Julie to turn it up a notch, and the blue eyed young blonde that everyone thought lived up to her hair color, strummed full on into the best damned version of "Orange Blossom Special" ever to be played on a guitar.

"YeeeeHAW!!" now THAT'S more like it!" Deb whooped as she grabbed Trish and the two of them two stepped into the night as the rest of the ladies clapped and whooped and hollered.

Green took this moment to quietly exit stage left. Moving quickly out of the firelight and into the darkness, he headed straight for Lucy's room.

Terry took this moment to whisk Marcie away from the firelight and off into the darkness, pulling them both up short just out of distance of the light from the bon fire, he stopped and kissed Marcie with a passion that she had never, ever felt before.

"Terry" Marcie said as she slowly pulled away, half wanting to stop this forward motion, and half not wanting to stop. "I...."

But Terry kissed her again, and again, until their tongues clashed together like the waves of the Hassayampa River during a monsoon.

He pulled away only long enough to move her further into the darkness and up against a tree where he continued to kiss her with a fire that burned right down into her soul.

"I need you, Marcie" Terry whispered as he stopped himself from taking this magnificent woman right then and there up against the tree he leaned her against. "I need you and I want you, but I won't do this here." He whispered as their mouths came together once more.

Marcie felt an aching deep down that she had long forgotten about with any man.... It was deeper than any sensual arousal could

140

produce, stronger than any passion could provoke. She was moved in a way she was no longer familiar with, and as Terry pulled back and held her chin up to him, looking right into her eyes, she realized the feeling she was experiencing, and before she could stop what was happening she whispered up to him the words she hadn't said in a hundred years.

"I love you" she quietly said. "I love you, Terry" she whispered again.

And as their lips crashed together once more, Terry slid his mouth down the side of her neck, flicking his tongue against her skin - moving back up towards her ear he whispered "Marcie, I have loved you since the day I laid eyes on you."

Turning her chin to him, his eyes bore deep into her soul as he said those three words again "I love you" and again "God help me I love you, and it is not my intention to let you go, Marcie. Stay here with me, let me know you better." He said, still looking deep into her eyes.

"Terry I ... I don't know know what to say, I wouldn't even know where to begin," she whispered.

"Then don't give me an answer yet, but promise me you will think about it. I don't want to get to know you through phone calls and emails, Marcie... I want to take this chance together, here on this ranch, you and me." He said as he traced the lines of her face with his hand, and kissed her gently one more time.

"I will Terry, I'll think about it, I ... oh God, is this really happening? I have to think about Lucy, but ... Terry - I ... I've never felt this way before. I don't know what to think right now, I just ..." her voice was lost as Terry pressed his lips to hers again and said, "just think about it, that's all I ask."

Terry pulled Marcie away from her leaning position on the tree, placed his arm around her side, and steered her in the direction of the ladies who were already wrapping up the evening with goodnights to each other.

"I see everybody is all smiles and still bright eyed and bushy tailed," Terry said to the group of women whose eyes were still twinkling from the light fun of the evening, and a few too many sips of what was left of the Chardonnay.

"You betcha!" Julie exclaimed through a wide grin and smiling eyes as she handed Terry his guitar.

141

"You sure surprised us with your strumming skills, little lady" Terry said to Julie.

"I've got all kinds of surprises underneath this skin o' mine!" Julie said as she stood up, stumbled and grabbed Deb's arm, who was also righting herself up from her own seat on a log. Giggling, the two gals straightened up and meandered towards their respective bunk rooms for the night.

Two by two and three by three or four, all the ladies except Marcie made their way back to their bunkhouses, making sure not one of them closed the door without hearing goodnight from each of them.

Their newfound friendships were becoming that sort of camaraderie, a rarity in the world they all lived in back at their own respective homes, in their lives where friendships were few and far between, and those that became close - only were when they needed something; and where not everyone was treated so equally as these women have treated each other, in the four short days they'd been at the Dusty Bar Trails Dude Ranch.

Chapter 18

Out of respect for Lucy's privacy, Green knocked gently on the door to the bunkhouse room she shared with her best friend.

"It's open, Marce" Lucy said softly.

"It's Green, Lucy … May I come in, please?"

A few seconds of silence passed by, and just as Green was about to step off the porch and head back to his own bunkhouse, he heard Lucy say "Yes, you can come in Green."

Green opened the door and stepped into the room, where Lucy was sprawled out on her bed in the prone position, arms dangling as she made circles with her fingers on the carpet on the floor by her bed.

"Hey there, beautiful" Green said quietly, as he sat on the bed beside her.

Lucy turned over, sat up, crossed her legs and inched closer to Green. On impulse Green put his arms around her and pulled her onto his lap, gently rocking her back and forth and kissing the top of her head, stroking her hair as he sat there quietly, waiting for her to speak.

"Green?" Lucy whispered.

"Yes, baby?" Green responded in a gentle tone.

"Please lock the door." She quietly requested.

"And can you please tell me how much longer I'll be married to that jerk, because Marcie left me hanging earlier." Lucy continued as Green unfolded himself and Lucy from the sitting position he was in, got up, walked across the room, and locked the door.

"Only if you admit that you left before she could finish, Lucy" Green said as he sat back down on the bed and pulled Lucy back onto his lap. She could feel his smile against the side of her head as he spoke.

"So you witnessed our antics, then?" Lucy said without looking up.

"I did" Green replied. "Really glad it ended without me having to pick up broken glass."

"Hmmm good point" she said.

"I admit I wouldn't let her finish, and that I left her standing there, Green, ok?" Lucy quietly said.

"Ok" said Green.

"Are you ready to hear this Lucy?"

"Are you still going to love me after I'm divorced, Green?"

"There is nothing that could make me stop loving you, beautiful."

"Then I'm ready"

Green took a deep breath and exhaled, kissed the top of Lucy's head again and gave her the information she was looking for.

"Two more days, Lucy honey. Just two more days" Green whispered to the now still woman in his arms.

After a few very long minutes ticked by, Green shuffled his body back towards the wall so that he could lean up against it, bringing Lucy with him and repositioning her on his lap.

"Will you lay down with me, Green? Will you lay here with your arms around me and let me let this sink in?"

"Will you stay here till my term us up, and come to Wyoming with me, Red?"

"I will, Green." Lucille whispered softly. "I will."

Without another word Green moved Lucy off of his lap, his arms still around her as he laid her down and nestled his body against hers.

"I don't think I can be loyal to him for two more days" Lucy whispered.

"I can understand that, Red ... but I don't want you to regret a single thing about our future, Lucy. So we'll wait." He whispered as he pulled her even closer up against him.

As the two lay together with their own thoughts, listening to the quiet of the night, Max jumped up on the bed, then climbed onto Green's hip, and stared him right in the eyes.

"I'll treat her right, Max" Green whispered to the old cat.

Max laid down on Green's hip, stretched his paws out, closed his eyes and began to purr.

"Is he kneading you?" Lucille asked. Green could tell she was smiling.

"He is"

"You ok with that?" Lucy asked.

"He's got pretty sharp nails, Red."

"You'll get used to it, Cowboy."

Green knew from the things that Marcie told him about Lucy's past, that Max hated Hank, and steered very clear of him. Green decided that there wasn't a chance in hell that he was going to lose this cat's trust, and that if his kneading went any deeper, there were bandaids in the kitchen.

And the two, (well… three,) fell fast asleep.

Leaving Wickenburg

Book 2

Follow Lucy and Green's new beginnings together, in March of 2019; and find out what Terry and Marcie have in store for their paths as well. See how the Wickenburg gang become a major and minor influence in all of their lives, and watch as an incredible story of love, empowerment, great friendships and magnificent times, unfold in the books to follow.

*Second chances only happen
if we have the belief enough in ourselves,
to see them*

Believe in yourself.

Press on.

Love and God Bless,

Amanda

Made in the USA
Coppell, TX
22 December 2023

26759992R00088